Mystic Moods

Short Stories of Rabindranath Tagore

Mystic Moods

Short Stories of Rabindranath Tagore

Translated by
Sinjita Gupta

UBSPD
UBS Publishers' Distributors Pvt. Ltd.
New Delhi • Bangalore • Kolkata • Chennai • Patna • Bhopal
Ernakulam • Mumbai • Lucknow • Pune • Hyderabad

UBS Publishers' Distributors Pvt. Ltd.

5 Ansari Road, **New Delhi**-110 002
Phones: 011-23273601, 23266646 • Fax: 23276593, 23274261
E-mail: ubspd@ubspd.com

10 First Main Road, Gandhi Nagar, **Bangalore**-560 009
Phones: 080-22253903, 22263901, 22263902 • Fax: 22263904
E-mail: ubspdbng@eth.net

8/1-B Chowringhee Lane, **Kolkata**-700 016
Phones: 033-22521821, 22522910, 22529473 • Fax: 22523027
E-mail: ubspdcal@cal.vsnl.net.in

60 Nelson Manickam Road, Aminjikarai, **Chennai**-600 029
Phones: 044-23746222, 23746351-2 • Fax: 23746287
E-mail: ubspd@che.ubspd.com

Ground Floor, Western Side, Annaporna Complex, 202 Naya Tola,
Patna-800 004 • Phones: 0612-2672856, 2673973, 2686170 • Fax: 2686169
E-mail: ubspdpat1@sancharnet.in

143, M.P. Nagar, Zone-I, **Bhopal**-462 011
Phones: 0755-5203183, 5203193, 2555228 • Fax: 2555285
E-mail: ubspdbhp@sancharnet.in

No. 40/7940, Convent Road, **Ernakulam**-682 035
Phones: 0484-2353901, 2363905 • Fax: 2365511
E-mail: ubspdekm@asianetindia.com

2nd Floor, Apeejay Chambers, 5 Wallace Street, Fort,
Mumbai-400 001• Phones: 022-56376922, 56376923
Fax: 56376921• E-mail: ubspdmum@mum.ubspd.com

1st Floor, Halwasiya Court Annexe, 11-MG Marg, Hazaratganj,
Lucknow-226 001• Phones: 0522-2294134, 2611128
Fax: 2294133 • E-mail: ubspdlko@lko.ubspd.com

680 Budhwar Peth, 2nd floor, Appa Balwant Chowk, **Pune**-411 002
Phone: 020-4028920 • Fax: 020-4028921
E-mail: ubspdpune@rediffmail.com

NVK Towers, 2nd floor, 3-6-272, Himayat Nagar,
Hyderabad-500029 • Phones: 040-23262572, 23262573, 23262574
Fax: 040-23262572 • E-mail: ubspdhyd@vsnl.net

Visit us at www.ubspd.com & www.gobookshopping.com

First Published 2005

Sinjita Gupta asserts the moral right to be identified as translator of this work.

All rights reserved. No part of this publication may be reproduced or transmitted in any form or by any means, electronic or mechanical, including photocopying, recording, or any information storage or retrieval system, without prior permission in writing from the publisher.

Cover Design: Dushyant Parasher

Printed at: **Sanat Printers, Kundli**

*I dedicate this book to the memory of
my dearest father Prof. Jitendra Mohan Sengupta and
my encouraging mother Smt. Protima Sengupta
who are no longer with me but whose
spiritual guidance rests in whatever I do.*

Acknowledgements

I would like to thank my uncle Shri Ajay Sengupta (Belu Kaku) for helping me with the original Bengali text and also my uncle Shri Parimal Dasgupta (Anshu Kaku) for encouraging me all the time and all the way. My sincere thanks are due to friends and well-wishers all over India. I remember with gratitude Prof. P Lal of Writer's Workshop who gave me the first impetus to write. I thank Mr Sukumar Das, Managing Director of UBS Publishers' Distributors Pvt. Ltd., for suggesting the wonderful idea of translating Tagore's works and of course Vivek Ahuja, the ever helpful Editor of UBS Publishers' Distributors Pvt. Ltd. I would be failing in my duty if I would not thank my husband Cmde. Swapan Kumar Gupta who helped me with compilation of the manuscript and my son Shoubhik for prodding me on.

Sinjita Gupta

Introduction

TAGORE'S UNIVERSE

His very name evokes awe and reverence. How could a man with no formal education living within the four walls of his ancestral house of Jora Sanko be blessed with such greatness of vision and such remarkable insight into human minds?

Once again proving perhaps that poets have a third eye—the inner vision which penetrates through innumerable barriers and brings out the hidden truth which lies within. We cannot but feel that here was born a seer—a man who was not of an age but one who had assimilated the ideas and feelings of all men of all ages into his creations and gained immortality in the field of art and literature.

Tagore's creative sphere was vast. There isn't any corner of artistic creativity that he has not touched. True enough, for does not the 'Ravi' or the Sun bestow brilliance to every sphere of life? Thus we witness the prophet and the visionary in his short stories, poems, dramas, novels or sketches. He analyses human emotions and aspirations, and sometimes weaknesses, with such dexterity and sympathy that we are left wondering—how could he guess? In Tagore's works the heavenly and the mortal interact and curiously mingle with each other to produce creations which remain alive and relevant for all ages and all times.

A marked characteristic to be noted in all his works is a sympathy for the oppressed and the ignored. In some cases his heart goes out for the underdogs of society like the poor farmer or the casual labourer or the old domestic servant struggling to make both ends meet. Sometimes this noble soul cries out for the women who have been kept under fetters for years and who have not learnt how to protest against such injustice. It is amazing how a person accustomed to the affluence of an aristocratic family background could put himself into the minds of people far removed from his stature and come up with such excellent analysis of characters and the society.

Tagore's short stories are like miniature novels with all the necessary ingredients of plot and characterisation. The only point which perhaps remains missing is the development of the plot-line over a larger period of time. Some of his novels like *Nashtaneer* or *Chokher Bali* are like further extensions of his short stories. Perhaps, as the Noble Prize winner for his poetry *Geetanjali* Tagore has gained more recognition as a poet and a dramatist. Tagore's stories keep us engrossed and at the same time deliver a subtle message. But the aesthetic quality is never sacrificed on the altar of didacticism. Every now and then we are treated to wonderful revelations of Nature and its influence on human moods, desires and aspirations. The lyrical beauty and poetic expressions manifest all over his creations speak volumes for the poet's intense love of Nature. Nature is presented as an omniscient force which works as a background to human emotions and everyday life.

Tagore and the Supernatural

We find a curious mingling of the real and the unreal in the works of Tagore. He seems to search for a link with the supernatural and the undiscovered all the time. Some of his short stories are excellent examples of Tagore's desire to know the unknown. Unfulfilled dreams, dead spirit longing to be in the company of the beloved who lives or sometimes forgotten pages of history coming alive, unrequited love seem to haunt the pages of his stories. *Golpoguchcho* or a bouquet of stories is a varied collection of social, supernatural, woman-oriented and children's stories. More than anything else, it is the conflict between the known and the unknown which faces us glaringly while reading them.

Rabindranath Tagore, in his personal life, had undergone several turmoils and tragedies. He had lost many of his children, his loving wife Mrinalini and his *bouthan* or elder sister-in-law Kadambari Devi with whom he shared a very special intimate relationship. His planchete ventures are well known. It would seem that Tagore had tried to establish a link with the world beyond death and had been drawn to the peculiar game of planchete where a dead soul is beckoned through a living medium and the words of the dead are recorded by a pencil which begins moving speedily as if prompted by a supernatural power. This desire to indulge in an imaginative communication with the dead might seem to be incongruous for a man of Tagore's stature, often termed by some as a kind of 'saintly immaturity'. His desire was prompted by some kind of an inner urge. His keen intellect rejected the thought yet his imaginative self revelled in this interplay of memory and oblivion. He neither accepted nor denied the existence of a life beyond death but was content to remain in that tottering sense of disbelief even though he wished to believe. Perhaps this was what the poet Coleridge had termed as a 'willing suspension of disbelief.'

When one goes through the records of some pencilled handwritten conversations between Tagore, his two consorts and the 'soul' of the dead, certain facts seem to astonish us. When he calls for his youngest son Shamindranath the medium writes like a child whereas the older 'souls' answer in perfect accordance with their specific images while alive. These have again aroused speculation regarding the medium—a young woman called Uma—and whether it was all a product of the sensitive girl's ultra-perceptive imagination. But how would this girl know certain intimate details of the relationship between Tagore and the dead souls close to his heart?

These questions perhaps remain unanswered. Tagore himself went through various stages of belief and doubt and the proof of this remains in the pages of the letters he would often write to Mrs Rani Mohalonabis in Calcutta. It is, however, interesting to note that Tagore's family had all along indulged in planchete and he had observed all these from his early years. He had, moreover, a marked interest in theosophical literature and subscribed to several magazines of such nature from around the world. Tagore and the supernatural is perhaps too vast and unfathomable a topic to discuss and speculate. But we may form an opinion of the true personality hidden within the poet—the sensitive and lonely man who knowingly and unknowingly indulges in fanciful imagination to pacify the deep urge to connect with his loved ones.

Tagore's Women

Tagore was a close observer of human emotions and aspirations. Hence it is not surprising that his stories deal with the problems facing women in society and how often they are forced to lead lives of utter depravation and disgrace. But as we talk of Tagore's conception of women we could recall what he had once said in his conversation with Dilip Roy—"Woman is not a man's competitor but his complement". To specify the essential nature of a woman's functions he exemplified, "a woman functions passively, subterraneously, like the roots of a tree, while man's fulfilment consists in spreading himself out like the branches through growth, adventure, activity." Or when he said, "Woman is so well saddled by Nature with qualities which man lacks like humility, restraint and self-abnegation"..... "Woman's need for emotion and earthwardness is greater than man's—while womanhood finds complete fulfilment through love and home, man's perfect fulfilment needs a more generous margin of freedom, of comparative detachment."

This very idea of women being the anchor of peace and stability in the turbulence of human emotions finds its expression in nearly all his heroines like Sucharita and Lolita, Kamala and Asha in *Naukadubi,* Lavanya in his exotic novel *Sesher Kabita* and, of course, Charulata in *Nashtaneer* or Binodini in the delightful treatise *Chokher Bali*. They represent the multiple facets of contemporary Bengali womanhood. The general mode of his characterisation is based on classical standards but has undergone several changes directed by the course of centuries. The older women like Rajlakshmi or Annapurna are generally of orthodox nature and yet cannot be termed as prototypes, for they differ widely among themselves. But the realist in Tagore made sure that essentially they should belong to a specific spectrum—that of middle-class Bengali society. Hence in Ketoki Mitra, or Katy Mitra as she calls herself, we find a typical product of the anglicised middle-class Bengali of those times. Through her ludicrous mannerisms, she creates an obnoxious sensation in the minds of the readers.

Talking of the women characters in his works, we remember Bimala in *The Home and the World* or Charulata in *Nashtaneer*. Tagore has revealed the intellectual and sensitive qualities which lie latent in women, unexplored and unappreciated. That a woman is not a mere embellishment of the household but also has an independent entity is shown by the writer in almost all his novels and short stories. The happiness and sorrows, the friction within and outside, the hopes and desires, conflict of ideology, individualism and national sentiments of this specific middle class are the subject of all his works. In the process, he has drawn out and enhanced the status of women in such a society.

About the book

One could go on and on talking about the enigma that is Rabindranath Tagore. I would not dare to venture beyond this. For this humble effort of trying to translate Tagore's short stories into English, I have chosen ten, some of which deal with the supernatural and some with women, while a few hint at mature man-woman relationships.

Craving Stones or *Khudito Pashan* is a vivid life-like depiction of dead souls haunting palatial mansions unrequited and unfulfilled. How a flesh and blood human being gets drawn to an imaginary illusory world of love and drama every night is the story narrated in this piece.

*Kanka*l or *The Skeleton* relates how the protagonist chances to meet a skeleton at night—the one which as a medical student he would use as an object of medical training. The skeleton happens to be that of a young beautiful woman who had committed suicide as her beloved, a doctor, had married someone else. The skeleton relates her sorrows to this man and disappears at dawn. The story dangles in a curious intermingling of belief and disbelief. *Manihara* or *Lost Jewels* is an intriguing and spine-chilling story of an avaricious, conceited, beautiful dead woman who comes back to haunt her husband's nights.

Nishithe deals with the guilt feelings of a husband who seems to hear his dead first wife's voice whenever he wants to get close to his second wife. *Jeevito O Mrito* or *The Living and the Dead* stresses on the fine line separating the natural and the supernatural and the irony of fate.

Darpaharan, *Samapti*, talk of some characteristic problems of man-woman relationships and also about social evils like the dowry system or social ostracism against the women or the marginalised. *Punishment*, *Penance* and *The Judge* deal with the themes of crime and punishment and love and justice.

All these ten stories have some messages to deliver though subtly hinted at. I myself have grown as a creative writer when as a translator I have groped for the right word, the suitable expression and subtle nuances of different shades of meaning. It has been a wonderfully enriching experience just trying to match the great master's expressions. Now I know why a 'translation' is often called a 'transcreation'. Any language loses a lot of its spontaneity when translated into another. It is perhaps outrageous to even attempt to translate the great master's works. I have tried to do so. If, in the process, I have digressed a bit it might be forgiven. I hope the stories have retained at least a part of their original flavour.

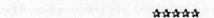

Contents

Acknowledgements vii

Introduction ix

1. Craving Stones 1
2. The Skeleton 18
3. In the Dead of Night 29
4. Lost Jewels 45
5. Metamorphosis 68
6. Punishment 96
7. Penance 111
8. The Judge 131
9. Humbling of Ego 142
10. The Living and the Dead 157

One

Craving Stones
Khudito Pashan

I met this character when my relative and I were returning to Calcutta by train after a long trip during the *Pujas*. I mistook him to be a Mohammedan from the West judging by his apparel. I was further puzzled after hearing him. He spoke so widely on different worldly topics that it seemed as though God consulted him before doing anything. We were quite happy not knowing how such unheard-of complicated matters were happening all over the world—that the Russians had progressed so much, that the British had harboured such secret designs and that the *rajahs* of our land had messed themselves up—all of these had happened to the complete blissful ignorance of us all. Our newly introduced friend smiled a little and said, "There happen more things in heaven and earth, Horatio than are reported in your newspapers."

We had recently been introduced to the world outside our homes and thus were bewildered at the ways and behaviour of this man. This man sometimes quoted science at the least excuse and sometimes explained from the *Vedas*, or sometimes suddenly quoted Persian couplets. Since we were not at all conversant with either science, the scriptures or the Persian language, our admiration for this man seemed to proliferate incessantly; so much so that my theosophist relative was firmly convinced that there was something uncanny associated with this co-traveller—some sort of magnetism or ethereal power, a spiritual presence or something of that nature. He was listening to the simplest of words uttered by this man with fervent admiration and noting them down secretly. I could say that even this unusual co-traveller could sense that and felt quite happy about it. When the train stopped at the junction, all of us got together in the waiting-room for the second train. It was ten thirty in the night. We heard that our train would be delayed due to some obstructions in the way. I had just decided to lay the bed scroll on the table to go to sleep when that stranger narrated this story which I now pen down. I could not sleep any more that night.

When I left my job at Junagadh due to some differences of opinion regarding administration and entered the ministry of the Government of Nizam in Hyderabad, I was first appointed as the tax-collector of the cotton crop in Barich since I was young and strong. Barich was a beautiful place. At the foot of the desolate hills, the Shusta river (the colloquial of Sanskrit *Swacchatoa*) ran though the large forests on the stony paths like an efficient dancer in fast, rhythmic movements meandering all along the way. On the banks of the river at the foothills stood a lonesome marble palace on the hundred-and-fifty-stepped low, stone platform. There was no habitation anywhere around. The cotton market and the village of Barich were far away.

Nearly two and half centuries back the second Shah Mahmud had built this palace in this desolate spot as a pleasure resort. The fountains in the bath would then shower rose-scented water and in that cool privacy, sitting on the etched out smooth marble, youthful Persian women would spread out their soft naked feet in the clear waters before going for a bath and sing the *ghazals* of the grapevine with the *sitars* on their laps and their hair let loose.

Now that fountain does not play any more, nor does the song; there are no dainty feet treading softly on the white marble any more—this is now a vast and deserted living accommodation for lonely, bachelor tax-collectors like us. But the old office clerk Karim Khan had warned me again and again against staying in this palace. He had said, "If you desire, you may stay during the day, but never stay here overnight." I had laughed it out. The servants said they would work only till the evening but would not stay overnight. I said it was all fine. This house had such a reputation that thieves too would not dare to venture here at night.

For the first few days I could feel the terrible burden of the loneliness of this discarded stone palace lie heavily on my heart. I would stay outside and work relentlessly as much as possible and return tired at night to retire.

But it was within a week that this house seemed to spread a magical web to ensnare me. I will not be able to describe my state of mind nor convince anyone about it. The entire house seemed to devour me into its enchanting womb and wear me out slowly as if it was a monstrous being.

Perhaps this process had started when I had stepped into this house, but I distinctly remember the day when I could feel its presence consciously for the first time.

Those days trade was low because of the advent of summer and I had no work that day. Just before sunset I sat on an easy chair placed on the lowest stone step of the river-bed. The river had dried up quite a bit, the sand bed opposite had coloured in the evening light, the stones in the shallow, clear water underneath the bank were shining. There was no breeze anywhere that day. From the hills nearby, a deep scent arose from the basil, mint and aniseed garden, and made the still air heavy with emotions.

As soon as the sun set over the top of the hills, a long curtain seemed to fall over the theatre of the day—there being a distance between the hills, the union of light and darkness did not linger for very long. I was about to get up to run around my house when suddenly I heard footsteps on the staircase. I turned back and saw—there was no one.

As I sat back thinking it was an illusion I heard the sound of many footsteps running down the stairs at the same time as if there were a number of people coming down together. A shiver ran down my spine along with a hint of glee. Although there was no figure before me, I could almost see clearly a vision as if on this summer evening a group of playful women had got down for a bath in the waters of the Shusta. Although in the evening hours there was no hint of a sound anywhere in the silent valley, river shore or the desolate palace, I could clearly hear the cheerful laughter of the women running for the bath, following each other, beside me as if a stream had just woken up from its sleep. They did not seem to notice me. I seemed to be as invisible to them as they appeared to me. The river was as still as before but I could clearly feel the shallow currents of the clear lake turning turbulent with the jingle of some bangled arms; some women splashing water on each other and the drops of water flying around like pearl drops all over the skies caused by delicate feet swimming and kicking at the water.

I could feel a tremble in my heart. Whether the excitement was from fear or joy or curiosity—I could not say. I strongly felt I should look clearly, but there was nothing to see in front. I felt I would hear them clearly if I strained my ears, but I could only hear the cry of the forest. When I tried to strain my ears, I felt, two-and-a-half centuries of a thick black curtain was flying right in front of me. I lifted it with a trembling heart and look in—there was a huge meeting going on there, but I could not see anything in the deep darkness.

Suddenly the still was broken by the outbreak of a strong breeze—the still waters of Shusta suddenly curled like the black hair of an *apsara** and the forests covered by the evening shadows all together and at the same moment seemed to wake up from a nightmare with a big murmur. Call it a dream or call it truth—an invisible illusion of two-and-a-half hundred years from the past which had appeared before me seemed to disappear in an instant. The illusory women who had passed along my side in their invisible form in quick footsteps and had run towards the Shusta waters in soundless, yet loud, chuckling laughter did not come back the same way wringing out their wet clothes. Just as the breeze blows the scent away, they too had been flown away by the deep breath of spring.

Then I was struck by a fear that perhaps Lady 'Poesy' had come and positioned herself upon me taking advantage of this loneliness. A poor tax-collector like me who lived by collecting taxes on cotton to be seized by this disastrous Lady to dwell on my poor head! I

---

* heavenly female dancer in Indian mythology

thought, I must eat well, for it is on an empty belly that all sorts of incurable diseases choose to attack a man. I called my cook and ordered him to cook rich and spicy authentic Mughlai food.

All these seemed ridiculous the next morning. I happily put on the pith hat, drove my car and whirled away for my investigative work. I was supposed to return late as this was the day for writing the tri-monthly report. But something began to draw me towards the house as soon as evening deepened. I cannot say what it was or who it was that pulled me towards it, but I felt that I should not delay any more. I felt as if all of them were waiting for me. I left the report incomplete, put on the pith hat and startling the dusty, shadowy and lonely road with the sound of my chariot wheels I reached that dark, silent and huge palace situated near the end of the forest.

The room facing the stairs was really large. The long-spread roof was supported by three rows of big pillars sculpted beautifully, which held back the ceiling. This huge room would resound with its endless emptiness all day and night. The lamp had not been lit even as evening had fallen. As soon as I pushed the door open and entered that huge room, sudden pandemonium seemed to break loose. It seemed as if some meeting had been disturbed and the participants fled away through doors and windows, the rooms, the path or the balconies; it was impossible to say where. I stood there surprised to find nothing at all. My body trembled with a feeling of enchantment. I could smell the essence of long-lost hair-fresheners and the soft fragrance of *aatar*.*
I stood there amidst the lamp-less, uninhabited

---
* perfume generally used by Muslims

chamber's ancient stone pillars, listening to the waters of the fountain sprinkling all over the white marble, some tune playing on the *sitar*,* which I could not fathom, somewhere the jingling of gold ornaments, the musical bells of anklets, at times the beating of the copper bell to announce the hour, sometimes the sound of *shehanai*† from afar, the sound of the hanging chandeliers moving in the breeze, the caged bird singing from the balcony, the pet stork crying out from the garden—all of these mingled to create an other-worldly atmosphere all around me.

I became so involved in this illusion that I felt this unfathomable, untouchable and unrealistic event was the only truth in the world and everything else a false mirage. That I was 'I' who gets rupees four-and-half hundred as salary for collecting tax on cotton, the 'I' who wears a pith hat and short waistcoat and goes to office in a carriage—all of these seemed to me such a strange, comical and unbiased falsehood that I stood there laughing loudly in the midst of that large, dark and immensely quiet room.

Right then my Muslim servant entered the room with a lit kerosene lamp. I cannot say whether he thought I was insane, but at that moment I suddenly remembered that I was Shri So and So, the eldest son of another Shri So and So. I even felt that only our greatest poets would be able to say whether there was really a living fountain forever gushing out from within this earth or somewhere outside; or whether some unseen fingers were striking at the illusory stringed musical instrument to create an 'eternal' melody—but this was without any doubt a definite fact that I received four-

---

* musical instrument
† musical instrument played in ceremonies considered auspicious

and-a-half hundred as salary for collecting taxes on cotton in the Barich market. At that moment, I smiled indulgently at the curious illusions created in me a few moments back and took up a newspaper sitting near the kerosene lamp-lit camp table.

After reading the newspaper and consuming the Mughlai dinner, I went to the tiny room in the corner, put off the lamp and lay down on the bed. I could see through the open window a sole, exceedingly bright star from the upper range of Araali mountains inspecting me attentively from the skies several crore miles far apart and I fell asleep marvelling amusedly. I do not know when or how long I had slept, suddenly at some point of time I woke up with a shiver; there had been no sound so far and I could not see whether someone had entered. The star from above the dark mountains had disappeared and the faint moonlight of the waning moon had entered through my window-pane in a way so as to show unwarranted hesitation.

I could not see anyone, but I still felt clearly as if someone was urging me very slowly to get up. As soon as I awoke the woman did not speak a word but signalled at me with her ringed five fingers and carefully ordered me to follow her.

I got up very quietly. Although there was not a single soul besides me in that hundred-chambered, immensely vacant, sleeping sound and walking-echoed huge palace, I could sense fear at every footstep of mine warning me not to awaken anyone else. The majority of chambers inside the palace would be shut and I had never been to any of them.

I will not be able to relate clearly today from where to where I went following the invisible, beckoning woman in silent footsteps and controlled breath that night. I travelled through so many narrow dark passages, several long balconies, so many sombre, silent, large meeting halls and so many suffocating secret chambers that I lost count.

Although I could not see my invisible messenger but her figure was etched in my imagination. She was an Arabian woman, her marble-sculpted arms could be seen through her open sleeves, a transparent veil covered her face hanging from the edge of her cap and there was a curved knife tied to her waistband.

I felt a special night had flown from the pages of the Arabian Nights and dissociated itself from the several hundred Arabian nights described there. I felt as if I had started out on a dangerous date through the narrow streets of sleeping Baghdad in this densely dark midnight hour.

At last my messenger stopped suddenly before a deep blue curtain and seemed to point her finger towards the ground. There was nothing there, but my blood curled up in fear. I could feel a horrifying African eunuch guard in a gown on the floor below that curtain sitting with an open sword on his lap and dozing off with both his legs stretched out. The woman messenger stepped across his legs lightly and lifted a corner of the curtain.

A part of a Persian carpet-spread room could be seen from within. I could not see who was seated on the throne. I could only spot the lower end of orange-hued, flared *pyjamas* where two small beautiful feet in *zari* slippers lay casually on the pink satin footrest. On the side of the floor lay apples, pears, oranges and several grape bunches in a bluish crystal vessel and, beside that, two small tumblers and golden wine in a glass decanter lay waiting for a guest. A wonderful intoxicating strong essence of some incense-stick seemed to waft in from the room only to enchant me.

As I tried to step across the stretched out feet of the sleeping guard with a trembling heart, he woke up with a start and the sword fell from his lap on to the floor with a loud noise.

Struck by a sudden horrible scream, I awoke to find myself sitting in the camp bed soaked in sweat, the crescent new moon turned into a pale complexion like a patient suffering from insomnia, and our madman Mehar Ali was shouting "Go away, go away" as was his regular routine every morning, and moving about the desolate path.

Thus ended a single night from my 'Arabian Nights' abruptly—but a thousand more nights were still to come.

My days were spent in constant tussle with my nights. I would go for work weary and tired during the day and would curse the illusory, magical night, but again in the evening my work-bound existence during the day would appear extremely small, insignificant, false and comical.

After dusk I would be wrapped up in the web of a peculiar addiction. I would transform into a beautiful character of some unwritten history enacted hundreds and hundreds of years ago. Then this foreign short coat and tight pantaloons did not suit me anymore. Then I would wear a red velvet cap, loose *pyjamas*, flower-embroidered *kaba* and long silk *choga*, pour essence into my coloured handkerchief, dress with great care, throw away my cigarette and take the rose-watered, many-curved long tobacco pipe and sit on a high seated big easy chair. I would wait for a wonderful meeting with my beloved at night with great eagerness and readiness.

Then as darkness deepened, strange events would take place which I would be unable to describe. It seemed as if some torn fragments of a great story would fly around like sudden breeze of spring inside these strange chambers of this huge palace. One could go somewhat but no further—one could not see the end. I too would follow those flying and revolving separated incidents and spend the night wandering around the chambers.

Amidst this part dream part reality—this sudden scent of *henna*, sudden sound of the *sitar*, sudden waft of breeze carrying the scent of perfumed water—I could see a heroine who would suddenly appear at moments like lightning. She was the one who wore saffron-hued *pyjamas* and her two soft, fair, reddish feet wore *zari* slippers curved at the tips, her breasts were covered with embroidered *zari* bodice, and she wore a red cap from which golden frills hung framing her fair forehead and cheeks.

She had turned me insane. Every night I would roam around the lanes and by-lanes and different chambers of an illusive existence through the dark depths of slumber, a dangerous path treaded in a trance.

On some evenings, when I would light up the two lights on both sides of the large mirror to dress up like an emperor with immense care, I would suddenly see the reflection of that young Iranian woman beside my reflection in the mirror. She would turn her well-formed chin in a moment, her black, large eyeballs would express deep, painful emotions with an enthusiastic side-glance, her juicy, beautiful cherry lips would seem to hint at something in an unsaid language, she would whirl her blossomed, youthful body in a light graceful dance movement upwards, spread feelings of pain, desire and temptation in a moment, rain sparks of laughter, meaningful glances and beautiful attire for a fleeting moment and then disappear into the mirror.

A daring breeze sweeping all the perfume from the hilly gardens would extinguish the two lights, I would change my attire, lie on the bed in the corner of the dressing room in a state of trance, charmed in body and mind, and shut my eyelids. Around me in the floating breeze and all the mixed scents of Araali hill gardens, I could feel several caresses, many kisses, palms touching softly, floating around covering the lonely darkness—I could hear many voices speaking, a scented breath would come upon my forehead and a soft lightly perfumed veil would come and touch my cheeks every now and then. It seemed as if, bit by bit, a magical, female serpent was trying to engulf my total being in its intoxicating embrace. I would drown myself in deep slumber, paralysed in body and spirit, after heaving a deep sigh.

On one such late afternoon, I decided to ride my horse to go out—I do not know who prevented me from doing so—but this time I did not pay heed to that. My British hat and short coat were hanging on the banister, I attempted to pull them out and wear them when suddenly a strong gush of stormy wind flew off the sands of the Shusta river and flagged the dry leaves from Araali hills and blew, spinning my coat and hat away, and a very sweet and playful, charming voice of laughter seemed to revolve with that breeze—hitting against all the strings of amorousness slowly rising from one level to a higher level and ultimately vanishing somewhere to the highest level near the setting sun.

I could not ride my horse that day and from the next day onwards I stopped wearing that short coat and British hat which had invoked such amusement.

That day around midnight I awoke to hear someone weeping in deep remorse and grief almost breaking the heart in two—as if someone was crying out from a deep, dark grave somewhere from below this bed, this floor and much below the stone foundations of this big palace and saying, "Please rescue me from here—from within this cruel magic spell, deepest slumber, unrequited dreams. Break open all the doors and pick me up on to your horse, hold me secure near your heart, ride through the forest, the mountains, the rivers and take me on to your sunlit rooms. Please rescue me!"

Who was I? How would I rescue someone? How would I pull out this unknown, drowning, desirable woman from the depths of this revolving, changing, dream world and get her ashore to reality? When did you exit, where did you live, oh heavenly beauty? In which cool oasis under the shadow of which date tree and of which nomadic desert woman were you born? Which Bedouin plunderer had torn you apart from your mother wild like a half-grown flower bud from the wild creepers, lifted you on a horse moving in lightning speed, crossed the burning sand desert and sold you in the slave market of which royal palace? The servant of which emperor had seen your shy, freshly bloomed youthful beauty there and bought you with gold coins, crossed the oceans, seated you on a gold chariot and presented you to the interior harems of his master's home? What history was enacted there? The music of that *sarangi*, the jingle of anklets and the flash of knives, the pangs of poison, the striking of sidelong glances amidst all that golden wine in a tumbler! What immense wealth, what an eternal prison! Two maids from both the sides fanning the emperor with leather fans and the diamonds in their bangles glittering like lighting! At the fair feet of the *Shahenshah* emperor lay his footwear embellished with jewels; the deadly looking *habshi* or eunuch guards stood at the entrance dressed up like angels carrying open swords in their hands. And then, how did you—you the flower bud from the desert—how did you swim through the blood-stained, jealousy-stricken, conspiracy-laden, violently illustrious oceans of wealth and power and how did you meet which cruel death and where, or were perhaps thrown into which more ruthless and more glorious shore?

Just then suddenly that madman Mehar Ali shouted out, "Run away, run away. It is all false." I looked to see that it was morning; the bearer handed me the post and the cook saluted me and asked, "What dinner should I prepare today".

I said, "No, I shall live in this house no more." The same day I collected my belongings and went to the office room. The old clerk of the office Karim Khan looked at me and smiled a little. I was annoyed at this smile and went on with my work without an answer.

As evening drew closer, I began to grow absent-minded. I felt I had to go somewhere—the checking of the account of cotton seemed absolutely unnecessary, even the governance of the Nizam did not appear very significant. Whatever was present, whatever was moving around, working or eating seemed to me extremely petty, meaningless and insignificant.

I threw away the pen, shut the huge ledger and immediately boarded my carriage to run back. I saw that my carriage stopped by itself at the appointed hour before dusk near the gate of that stone palace. I ran up the stairs and entered the room.

Today, there existed an overbearing silence. The dark rooms seemed to be cross with me and appeared glum.

My heart swooned with remorse, but I did not know who to tell and whom to ask for forgiveness. I roamed around the dark chambers with a heavy heart. I was struck with a desire to pick up any musical instrument and sing a song to someone, and say, "Oh Fire, the moth which had tried to escape from you has come back to die again. Just excuse him this time, burn his two wings, burn him totally."

Suddenly from somewhere on the top a few drops of tears seemed to fall on my forehead. That evening the hilltops of Araali had been thickly covered with dark clouds. The dark forests and the still black waters of the Shusta seemed to await a fierce arrival. The earth and the sky suddenly trembled; and without any warning, a crazy storm seemed to reveal lightning-like fangs, threw open its chains and ran through the dense, far forests screaming like an insane man. The doors of the large, empty chambers of the palace seemed to beat against each other, crying out in terrible pain.

The servants were all in the office room and there was no one who could light up the palace. On that cloudy, new-moon night in the deep, dark interiors of the palace, I could feel clearly—a woman had turned face down on the carpet at the foot of the bed and was tearing her loose tresses, pulling at them with her tight fists, her fair forehead was bursting into blood. Sometimes she was laughing fiercely in a low, dry tone, and sometimes aloud, she was weeping inconsolably, at time groaning and at times crying fiercely. She had torn open her bodice with her own hands and was beating upon her bare bosom, the storm was roaring out from the open window and severe rain had come inside and was wetting her all through.

The storm did not stop that entire night, neither did the weeping. I wandered around the chambers in unfulfilled remorse and regret. No one was there. Who could I console, whose was this violent sorrow? From where did this turmoil of remorse originate?

The madman cried, "Run away, run away. All this is false, this is false." I saw that it was dawn and Mehar Ali, as was his practice, was crying out his habitual warning after circling the palace, even in this inclement weather. Suddenly I thought perhaps Mehar Ali had lived in this palace sometime like me, and even though he had turned mad he would come back to this palace every morning attracted to the grave charms of this stone-giant.

I immediately ran to the madman in the rain and asked him "Mehar Ali, what is false, tell me?"

He did not answer and pushed me back and wandered around the house like a whirling bird caught in the fangs of a great serpent moving in a trance-like spell. But again and again he would warn himself by saying, "Go away, go away, all is false, all is false."

I ran crazily through the storm and asked Karim Khan in office, "What is the meaning of this, open up and tell me."

What the old man said added up to this. "Once upon a time that palace had been a witness to a host of unfulfilled desires; many violently passionate and lustful encounters had shaken its foundation—each of the stone pieces of this palace is hungry and thirsty with those heartburns and unrequited desires of cursing souls who want to devour any living person like a craving monster. Whoever has spent three nights in that palace has not succeeded in breaking out of its clutches except for Mehar Ali who had run out of the palace, totally insane."

I asked, "Will I never be able to escape?"

The old man said, "There is only one solution. But the ways are very difficult. I will tell you everything; but before that I must tell you the old history of an Iranian slave woman of Gulbagh. There has never happened a stranger and more heart-rending incident in this world... ."

Just then the porters came and said, "The train is coming." So soon? The train arrived while we were packing the bedding. An Englishman just awakened in the first-class compartment of the train was trying to read the name of the station peeping out from the window. Seeing our co-passenger friend, he cried out, "Hello," and then picked him up. We boarded the second class. We never came to know who the man was, neither did we hear the end of the story.

I exclaimed that the man had completely fooled us assuming that we were simpletons and the story was totally fabricated. Because of this very argument, I have thereafter severed all connections with my theosophist relative.

Two

The Skeleton
Kankal

The room beside the one where we three childhood friends slept had a full, grown human skeleton hanging on the wall. The bones would sway in the night breeze, making a clattering noise. In the daytime we had to 'clutter' those very bones. Those days we would read *Meghnadvadh Kavya**, the Bengali epic written by Michael Madhusudan Dutt, from our Sanskrit teacher and learn osteology from a student of Campbell School. Our guardian wished to make us experts in all types of subjects. How far he had succeeded in his mission would be unnecessary to describe to people who know us well, and best to keep a secret from people who do not.

A long period had passed by since then. All this while, no one could discover where the skeleton from that room and osteology from our heads had disappeared.

A few days back I had to sleep for a night in that room as for some reason there was a scarcity of space elsewhere. I was not able to get sleep there as I was not accustomed to it. Turning from one side to another, I could hear the church bells ringing one by one. At this moment the oil lamp, which was burning at a corner, flickered for about five minutes and extinguished totally.

---

* a Bengali epic written by Michael Madhusudan Dutt—a landmark in Indian poetry written in epic style

Our family had experienced one or two tragedies before this. Thus as soon as the light went off, I naturally thought of the blackness of death. I felt that, just as this flame of light had disappeared into eternal darkness at this late hour of the night, the tiny little flames of human life which are extinguished and lost forever sometimes during the day or sometimes at night would appear to be of the same magnitude in the eyes of Nature.

Gradually, I remembered the 'skeleton'. Thinking of its living state suddenly I felt as if a living object was trying to find its way in the dark, catching hold of the wall of the room and moving around my bed. I could hear the heavy breathing. It seemed as if it was searching for something, but not getting it and circling round the room at a faster pace. I understood for sure that all this must be my sleepless, excited brain's imaginative fancy, and the blood running fast in my head must be creating a peculiar sort of noise which seemed to sound like quick footsteps. But, even then, my body trembled with fear. I tried forcefully to dispel this unnecessary fear and said, "Who is that?" The footsteps stopped near my mosquito net and I heard a reply, "It's me. I have come to search for my skeleton which has disappeared."

I thought, threatening one's imaginative creation was not very difficult, so I caught the pillow tightly and spoke naturally in a familiar tone—"You have found a good job at this time of the night. Now, what do *you* need that skeleton for?"

The reply came from very close to my mosquito net, "What do you mean? My chest bone lies there itself. Twenty-six years of my youth had blossomed around that—would I not like to see it?"

I immediately said, "Yes, yes. What you say is quite justified. Why don't you go and search? I will try and get some sleep in the meanwhile." It said, "Are you alone? Then I will sit with you. Let us talk. Thirty-five years back I too would sit with human beings and converse with them. All these thirty-five years I have only wailed along the winds blowing in graveyards. Today let me sit near you and talk to you once more as a flesh and blood human being does."

I felt someone come and sit near my mosquito net. Seeing no other alternative, I said with somewhat more enthusiasm, "That's better. Say something which will make us happier."

The church bell chimed twice—it was two a.m. "When I was a flesh and blood human and younger of age, I would fear one person more than death itself. He was my husband."

"I would feel the same as what a fish feels when it is caught in a fisherman's net. I would feel as if some completely unknown, strange creature was baiting me out from the deeply affectionate waterbed of my birthplace to snatch me far away—I would never be able to escape him. Barely two months after my wedding, my husband died. My relatives mourned and regretted on my behalf as much as possible. My father-in-law examined several astrological phenomena and told my mother-in-law, 'This girl is what is called a 'cursed woman' in the sacred books.' I clearly remember those words. Are you listening? How does it sound?"

I said, "Interesting. The beginning of the story is quite intriguing."

"Then listen. I returned to my father's place happily. I began to grow in years. People would try to keep it a secret from me but I knew very well that one did not find such a beautiful woman as me easily anywhere and everywhere."

"Quite possible. But I have never ever seen you." "Didn't you see? Why, haven't you seen that skeleton of mine? Hee, hee, hee, hee! I am just kidding. How can I prove to you that there were once two large, expressive, jet black eyes in those two hollow eyeholes and that soft smile which would play upon those cherry lips can never be imagined when one sees the hollow, bare set of teeth along with that horrific grin which appears on them today? How can I describe to you the grace, the beauty and the firmly built yet, soft and supple youthful fullness which was blossoming day by day—covering up those few, long, dry pieces of bone which you have witnessed? Even the established doctors of those days would find it hard to believe that one could study osteology from that 'beautiful' body of mine. I know, a doctor had called me a *kanak-chapa** confiding to a special friend of his. The meaning of all this would be that all the rest of the people in this world were samples to be studied in osteology and physical exercise, while only 'I' was like a *kanak chapa* symbolising eternal beauty. Can you search for a skeleton in a *kanak chapa?*"

"When I would walk I could feel myself how, at every step I would generate a variety of lovely expressions manifesting themselves as the billowing waves of an ocean, just as when a piece of diamond is turned on all its sides it exudes brilliance all around lighting up the surroundings. I would gaze at both my arms for hours—such two arms could sweetly tie the reins on all the arrogant masculinity of this world and hold them tight very easily. When Subhadra had driven Arjun† in her triumphant chariot blazing all through

---

* *a* golden hued flower found in Bengal
† two characters from *Mahabharata*—Arjun was the brave Pandava prince known for his skilled archery and Subhadra his female consort

the stunned three worlds, perhaps she too would have possessed two such slender, crimson-hued, perfectly shaped arms, pinkish palms and fingers like flames of charming elegance."

"But that shameless, bare, naked, forever-aged skeleton of mine is bearing false witness to my words. I was unable to defend my case then. That is why, my anger is directed most against you. I feel that I should present before you the same woman blessed with sixteen springs—full of life, flushed with youth and hot-blooded—and banish sleep from your eyes for life and drive away osteology from your brain forever."

I said, "If you were living, I would have touched you and sworn I am not thinking a bit of osteolgoy right now. And that bewildering, abundantly youthful beauty of yours has been etched out so brightly upon the dark canvas of the night! You need not say any more."

"I had no companion. My elder brother had sworn that he would never marry. I would live alone in the interiors of the house. I would sit underneath the trees in the garden all by myself and think—the world around loves 'me' only, all the stars above are examining 'me', the passing breeze is sighing again and again and under some pretext hovering all the time around 'me'—and perhaps, if the grass bed on which I had spread my feet ever came to life, it would become inanimate once more at my touch. I would imagine that all the young men of this world were waiting silently at my feet in a long queue quite like these grass beds waiting to hold my feet; and would feel a tug at my heart for no apparent reason.

When my brother's friend Shashishekhar passed out from the Medical College, he took over the responsibility of being our family doctor. I had seen him quite often earlier, although secretly. My elder brother was a strange person—he never seemed to observe the world consciously. It would appear as if this world was not spacious enough for him—he had dissociated himself further and further from it almost till the end point.

He had only one friend, Shashishekhar. Hence I would only meet this Shashishekhar—the only one among the entire lot of young men outside my home in the wide, wide world.

And in the evening when I would sit under the flower tree like an empress on her throne, the entire male species of the world would take on the semblance of Shashishekhar and grovel at my feet. Are you listening?"

"What do you think?" I sighed and said, "I was thinking it would be great to be born as Shashishekhar".

"Listen to the story first. One rainy day I was lying with fever. The doctor had come on his visit. That was our first meeting."

"I was lying facing the window so that the red hues of the evening light should colour the pallor on my sick face. When the doctor entered the room and glanced at my face I imagined myself to be him and looked at my own face. A slightly pained petal—soft face, unrestrained locks of hair falling on the forehead and shyly lowered long eyelashes drawing shadows on the cheeks. The doctor said politely in a soft tone, 'I must check the pulse'".

"I stretched out a weary, rounded arm from within my clothes. I glanced at my arm once and thought if I could wear blue glass bangles it would look even more appealing. I had never seen a doctor more hesitant to see the pulse of a patient ever before. He felt the degree of my temperature. I too could sense how the pulses of his heart were moving. Don't you believe?"

I said, "I do not find any reason not to—pulse rates of a human may vary from time to time."

"In course of time, after falling ill and recovering a few more times, I felt that slowly, in that imaginary gathering of mine, the number of males was reducing from a few crores to a single one—my world almost shrunk and grew sparsely populated. There remained for me only one doctor and one patient in this wide, wide world."

"I would secretly wear a yellow shaded saree in the evening, tie a perfect bun with my hair and wound a bunch of *beli** flowers around it, hold a mirror in hand and sit in the garden."

"Why, can anyone be totally satisfied seeing oneself? Positvely, never. Because, I would never see myself as myself. I would sit down alone and yet think like two. I would then be the doctor and see myself through his eyes—would be bemused by myself, love and caress myself, but a deep sigh within me would blow across like the evening breeze."

"From then onwards I was alone no longer; when I would walk I would look down and see how my feet were treading on the earth and think how this movement would appear to the eyes of this newly passed-out medico; the afternoon sun would blaze outside the window, there would be no noise anywhere, sometimes a kite would fly farther into the skies making a peculiar sound; and just beyond our garden wall, a toy seller would cry 'Toys, toys, bangles for sale' in a musical note, and I would spread a sparkling white

---

* a perfumed white flower akin to the jasmine found in summer months in India worn in small garlands round the hair

bedsheet, make my own bed and lie there alone. I would spread out a bare arm as if carelessly on the soft bed and think; perhaps someone would see this arm of mine resting in this particular manner, and would take my arms in his hands, someone would plant a kiss on the pinkish palm and go back again slowly, very slowly Just think if the story ends now, how will it be?"

I said, "Not bad. It would be a little incomplete, of course, but I could spend the rest of night trying to figure out the conclusion. But then the story would turn far too serious. Where would the humour be? Where will the skeleton inside display itself baring forth its sets of teeth?"

"Then listen to what happened next. After earning a reputation, the doctor opened his practice in a chamber in the ground floor of the house. I would sometimes ask him jokingly about medicines, poisons, what made a person conk off easily—all such matters. The doctor, enthused by such questions on medical science, spoke a lot about them. Hearing him speak, I seemed to get myself closely acquainted with death. 'Love' and 'death'—I saw only these all around me and everywhere in this world."

"My story is about to end—there is only a little left."

I said softly, "The night too is about to end."

"From few days I had observed that the doctor was very absent-minded and seemed to be rather embarrassed whenever he met me. Once I saw that he had dressed up a wee bit too much and had asked for the carriage from my elder brother—he had to go somewhere in the evening. I could stay no longer. I went to my brother and after discussing many other topics, broached this topic. I asked him, 'Brother where is the

Doctor Babu going—why has he asked for the carriage?' My brother replied briefly, 'To die.' I said, 'No, please tell me the truth'. He clarified his earlier statement and said, 'To get married'.

I said, 'Is that true?' and began to laugh aloud. Soon I came to know that the doctor would receive twelve thousand rupees as dowry for the marriage."

"But what was the significance of keeping it a secret from me, thereby insulting me? Had I caught his feet and pleaded that I would die of heartbreak if he did this? You can never trust the males. I have met only one man in this world and have received all this knowledge within seconds of this meeting.

When the doctor arrived home after visiting patients just before evening, I laughed and laughed before asking him, 'So, doctor sir, I believe today is your wedding'.

'Seeing my happy spirits, the doctor seemed to appear not only rather embarrassed, but quite sad.

I asked him, 'But where is the orchestra and band?'

He heaved a small sigh and said, 'Is the event of a marriage so very joyous?'

I was beside myself roaring with amused laughter and told him, I had never ever heard of such a thing. I said, 'This won't do; there has to be an orchestra, there have to be bright lights.'

I harried my brother so much that he immediately got busy with suitable wedding arrangements.

"I went on with my conversation with him—What would happen when the bride would come, what I would do. I asked, 'Tell me Doctor, would you carry on checking the pulses of patients even then?'

Hee hee! Hee hee!"

"Although the minds of human beings, especially those of the male species are not quite visible, I could swear that my words were striking the heart of the doctor like thunderbolts."

"The auspicious hour for the wedding had been fixed for late night. In the evening the doctor was sitting on the terrace with my elder brother and drinking one or two pegs. Both of them were used to this. The moon appeared overhead."

"I came in laughingly and said, 'I hope you haven't forgotten, Doctor? It's high time you started for the wedding venue.'"

"Here I must tell you a small thing. In between I had gone to the chamber, collected some powder and mixed a part of that in the glass of the doctor at my convenience and without anyone's notice. I had learnt from the doctor himself which of the powders could kill a person if consumed."

"The doctor gulped the remains in the glass and said in a slightly softened and emotionally heightened voice glancing at me with a heart-wrenching look, 'So, I must say goodbye.'"

"The flute began to play, I draped a *Benarasi* sari,* took out all the jewellery which was preserved in the iron chest, bedecked myself and applied thick vermilion to my hair parting. I laid my bed underneath that *bakul*† tree."

"It was a beautiful full-moon night glowing with snowy light. The southern breeze was blowing, driving away all the troubles of the sleeping world. The fragrance of the jasmine and *beli* flowers had covered the entire garden."

---

* rich bridal silk sari designed in Benaras, holy city in Northern India
† perfumed flower found in Bengal

"When the sound of the flute slowly faded far away, and the moonlight changed to darkness, when the trees and the sky and the world of my well-known home and town seemed to slowly disappear from around me like an illusory dream, I closed my eyes and smiled."

"My wish was that when people would come and see me this bit of a smile would linger drowsily upon my lips like a sweet dream."

"My last wish was that when I would enter my wedding chamber of the eternal night with slow, hesitant footsteps, I would carry this smile along playing upon my lips. But where was the wedding chamber? Where was my bridal attire? I woke up with a cluttering sound somewhere within me and saw, three boys studying osteology with my bones. In my chest where my heart would beat with joy and sorrow and youthful petals of my dreams would blossom everyday one by one, a master stood pointing a cane and teaching his pupils the name of each bone in the bone-cage there. And that last bit of smile, which I had presented so carelessly on my lips—did you see any sign of it?"

"How did you like the story?"

I said, "The story is quite absorbing."

At this moment, the first crow of dawn cawed. I asked. "Are you still there?"

I did not receive any answer. The early morning rays entered the room.

☆☆☆☆☆

Three

In the Dead of Night
Nishithe

Doctor! Doctor!

What a nuisance! A call at this hour! I woke up only to see that it was our landlord Dakshinacharan Babu. I scrambled up and pulled in the bench with broken backrest for him to be seated and looked up to his face with a worried glance. I glanced at the clock. It was half past two in the night.

Babu Dakshinacharan spoke with a pale face and dilated eyes, "This night there has been a similar kind of predicament. Your medicine has not worked at all."

I answered, a little hesitantly, "Perhaps you would have had a drink too much".

Dakshinacharan Babu spoke with utmost annoyance, "That is of course your biggest blunder. The cause is not alcohol, you would not be able to guess what it is unless you hear about it all from the beginning to the end."

There was a kerosene lamp placed in a tiny tin box burning faintly. I moved it a bit so that there was some more light all over, along with a lot of smoke. I pulled my *dhoti** around myself and sat on a packing box covered with newspaper. Dakshinacharan Babu spoke thus:

---

* Indian dress worn in a particular style around the waist generally of cotton material

A perfect housekeeper like my first wife one rarely came across. But I was quite young, easily moved emotionally and, on top of that, had studied poetry well. Thus such perfect housekeeping did not quite fulfil my cherished romantic ideals. I was often reminded of the poet Kalidas's couplet which said,

> *Grihini sachivaha sakhi Mithah*
> *priya Sisya lalite Kalavidhau*

(A wife is a friend, confidante, loving disciple to groom in the art of love.)

But none of Kalidas' words on romantic art seemed to apply to my wife. If I ever tried to address her as a beloved she would laugh it off. Just as Lord Indra's heavenly elephant *Aairavat** had been washed away along with the flowing Ganges, all my great poetic enterprises and sweet, loving addresses would be washed away in a moment of dismay when she laughed at them. She exuded a strange power when she laughed in her scornful way.

Thereafter, about four years back I was attacked by a dangerous illness. I almost died due to lip blisters and heavy delirious fever. I had lost all hopes of living. Once it so happened that the doctor too resigned to fate. But suddenly, from somewhere a relative of mine fetched a monk who fed me some type of a herb ground with home-made butter. I was saved then—whether it was the medicine or it was my destiny to live, I do not know.

---

* A Hindu mythological creation; an elephant with magical powers. Here it refers to an incident in mythology where the King of the Heavens Lord Indra had been defeated in war and his faithful, magical elephant Aairavat had been washed away by the River Ganges

All through my illness, my wife had not rested even for a moment. During those days this weak woman had fought with all the messengers of death who had assembled at my doorstep with her humanly powerless strength and immense eagerness and anxiety. She had protected my undeserving life like a mother holds a baby to her breast with her two arms showering all her love, her entire being and her utmost care. She thought of nothing else in this world—neither food nor slumber—but my well-being.

The Lord of Death then released me from his clutches like a defeated tiger, but before leaving struck his deadly claws severely on my wife.

My wife was pregnant then; soon she gave birth to a stillborn child. Thereafter, a series of complicated diseases seemed to strike my wife. Now, I began to nurse her. She would feel embarrassed at this and say, "Oh! What are you doing—what will the world say. Don't you come and go into my room all through the day and night."

Sometimes I would try to fan her during the night when she was ill-pretending to fan herself, but it would all end in a fitful struggle between her and me as to who should fan whom. If ever I would try to nurse her and in the process get delayed for my regular lunch timings by even ten minutes—it would become the reason for several requests, pleadings and complaints from her. My good intentions would often backfire. She would say, "A man should never go to such extremes."

I think you have seen our house in Baranagore. There is a garden facing it and the Ganges river flows in front of it. Just below our bedroom there lies a plot of land towards the south, which my wife had converted to a small garden of her personal choice and covered it up with a fencing of *henna* plants.

Of the entire garden, this plot of land was the most ordinary and extremely homely. That is, there were none of those showy, essence-less colourful flowers nor a variety of leaves rather than flowers, and neither were those insignificant creepers in the pots with sticks carrying Latin names on papers flying like victory banners. There were Chinese jasmines, roses, tuberoses, the *jessamine*, the *gardenia* and the *oleander*, growing in abundance. There was white marble-build platform at the base of the huge *bakul** tree. When she was fine, she would stand there and wash it herself. That was her seat of leisure during summer evenings. She could see the river but the *babus* strolling in their luxury yachts in the river could not see her.

After long bedridden days, one *Chaitra*† moonlit night she said, "I am feeling suffocated in this closed room. I would like to sit for once in that garden of mine." I helped her up with utmost care, very slowly, and laid her on the marble platform underneath the *bakul* tree. I could have placed her head on my lap, but I knew she would consider it strange behaviour. Therefore I placed a pillow underneath her head.

One or two blossoms of *bakul* flowers showered all around and a shadowed moonlight seemed to fall on her frail face from somewhere behind its branches. There was a quiet silence all around. Sitting quietly there on the other side in that heavily shadowy darkness, I looked at her face and my eyes moistened with tears.

I slowly came nearer and caught hold of one of her warm, feverish shrivelled hands with mine. She did not

---

* a flower grown in Bengal
† last month in the Bengali Calendar

object. After a short while of stillness, my heart seemed to take a turn and I said suddenly, "I will never forget your love".

At once I felt I need not have uttered those words. My wife laughed aloud. A sense of shyness, pleasure, a little mistrust and also a great deal of sharp sarcasm underlined her laugh. She never spoke a word of protest, but through that laugh of hers she seemed to say,"You will never forget—that is quite impossible and I never expect that."

I had never dared to discuss serious romantic matters with my wife because of that sweet yet sharpened laughter of hers. Whatever arose in my mind in her absence would vanish when I met her and seemed like utter rubbish. The words which bring tears to one's eyes when read in print somehow always appear ridiculous when we try to utter them.

One can argue with statements but there can be no debate over laughter. Thus, I had to stop. The full-moon night grew brighter and a cuckoo kept on cooing constantly. I sat and kept on thinking why the cuckoo's mate was deaf to its cries even on such a moonlit night.

My wife never showed any signs of improvement even after a lot of treatment. The doctor said, "A change might work wonders." I set forth for Allahabad with my wife.

Here, Dakshinababu stopped suddenly. He looked at my face suspiciously, and then caught hold of his head between his hands and began to think. I too kept mum. The kerosene lamp was dimly lit in a box and the buzzing of mosquitoes was quite audible in that silent room. Suddenly Dakshinababu broke the silence and began his story once again.

There Doctor Haran began treating my wife.

At last after a long period of treatment, the doctor too said, I also understood as well as did my wife, that this ailment could not be healed. She would have to live forever ailing and sickly.

Then one day my wife told me, "I will not recover and there is no chance of my dying soon. How long can you lead a life with this decaying being? Do marry once more."

Her words appeared to be a piece of logical good advice—they were not uttered like a great declaration of nobility or heroism or anything extraordinary like that.

It was my turn to laugh. But could I laugh as she did? I spoke like the hero of a novel—solemnly and dramatically—"As long as I live... ." She stopped me and said, "Come on now, say nothing further—I do not know what to say,"

I admitted defeat and said, "I will never love another in my life". She laughed aloud at my words. Thus, I had to stop.

I do not really know whether I had ever openly admitted to myself, but the fact seems clear to me now, now that I had grown weary of this futile, hopeless, nursing both in mind and spirit. That I could ever forsake my duty; I could never dream, but that I would spend my entire lifespan with an ever sickly person appeared terrible.

Alas! When I had looked forward in the first flushes of youth—the future wrapped up in illusions of love promises of fulfilment and mirages of beauty had seemed so glorious; today, it seemed that till the end of my sojourn it was a hopeless, terribly long and parched desert.

My wife would surely have observed that inner fatigue underlying my nursing. I did not know then but I do not have any doubt now that she could read me easily quite like the first few alphabets at the primary level. Hence whenever I would address her as the hero of a novel—all poetic and dramatic—she would laugh it off in inevitable amusement and a deep affection. Even today the realisation that she knew of my unspelt, innermost, secret thoughts all along fills me with utter shame.

Haran doctor was from a caste similar as mine. I would be invited quite frequently to his house. After a few days, the doctor introduced me to his daughter. The girl was unmarried—she would be about fifteen. The doctor said he could not get his daughter married as he could not find a suitable groom. But I would hear strong rumours that there was some kind of blemish in her family history.

But there was no other defect in her. She was as accomplished as she was beautiful. Thus I would often return home late at night after discussing all kinds of topics with her, and would often miss the hour of feeding my wife her medicines. She knew, that I had gone to Doctor Haran's house but she never ever asked me the reason for the delay.

I began to see mirages of an oasis once more in this desert-like life. When my heart was drying with thirst, there was an abundance of clear water gurgling and overflowing its limits before my eyes.

The room of the patient now began to appear doubly more dreary and stifling. The daily chores of nursing and feeding medicines would often be disturbed.

Doctor Haran would often tell me that, for the ones who had no hope of revival, death was a better alternative. There was no happiness for themselves and they were a burden to others. There was no harm talking about such issues but I felt he should not have broached this topic pointing to my wife. Or else was it that the minds of doctors were so insensitive to matters of life and death that they failed to understand our feelings?

Suddenly one day I heard my wife telling Doctor Haran in the next room, "Doctor, why are you prescribing so many medicines just to increase the medical bill? When my life itself is an illness, why don't you prescribe a cure so that it is released very soon?"

The doctor said, "Tch! Tch! Please do not utter such words".

The words struck hard at my heart. I went to her room after the doctor left and sitting on the edge of her bed, stroked her forehead slowly. She said "This room is very warm you go out for a while. This is the time for your outing. Your appetite will suffer if you do not go out for a walk." My walk meant going to the doctor's residence. I was the one who had explained to her that it was very necessary for me to go for a walk in order to increase my appetite. Now I can say for sure, she understood my deception well. I was foolish to think that she was foolish.

Thus saying Dakshinacharan Babu sat for a long time resting his head on his palm. Thereafter, he said, "Bring me a glass of water". After that he began to say.

Once Manorama, the daughter of the doctor, expressed a desire to see my wife. I do not know why I did not like this proposal of hers. But I did not know how to say no to her. She appeared one evening at my house.

That day may wife's pain had worsened compared to other days. She would be extremely quiet and still when her pain aggravated; only sometimes her fists would close tightly and her face turned bluish in colour, giving a hint of her excessive agony.

There was a dead silence in the room. I was sitting quietly at the bedside. She did not even have the strength to ask me to go for a walk that evening or perhaps she wished that I should stay with her when she was suffering so. The kerosene lamp had been kept near the door to keep away from the eyes. The room was dark and soundless. One could only hear sometimes the deep sighs of relief from pain that my wife occasionally breathed.

Just then Manorama came and stood near the open doorway. The light of the lamp fell on her face from the opposite side. In that melee of light and darkness she could not see anything inside the room and stood hesitantly at the doorway.

Startled, my wife caught my hand and asked, "Who is *that*?" In her weak state, scared to see a stranger, she asked me softly, two or three times, "Who is that? "Who is *that*? Dear?"

Suddenly overcome by some evil thought, I began to say, "I do not know." As soon as I uttered this I was whiplashed by my conscience. I blurted out, "Oh! It is only the daughter of the doctor".

Manorama came and sat in the room. Some conversation went on between her and my ailing wife. Soon the doctor arrived.

He had brought two bottles of medicine with himself. He took them out and told my wife, "This blue bottle contains massage oil and the other should be administered orally. Beware, do not mix up the two; for one is deadly poison."

He warned me once more and kept the two bottles side by side on the table by the bedside. While leaving the home, the doctor called his daughter. Manorama said, "Father, why don't I stay? There is no woman with her. Who will nurse her?"

My wife hurriedly said, "No no, please do not worry. The old maidservant here looks after me like a mother." The doctor smiled and said, "She is like the Goddess Lakshmi. She has always nursed others, she cannot accept nursing from others."

The doctor was about to depart with his daughter when my wife said, "Doctor, he has been sitting in this enclosed room for a long time. Could you please take him out in the fresh air?"

The doctor told me, "Come on, Sir, let me take you along the riverside."

I agreed after an initial short-lasting refusal. The doctor warned my wife about the two bottles of medicine once more before leaving.

I had my dinner at the doctor's house that night. I returned late at night to find my wife suffering acutely. Struck with regret, I asked, "Has your pain aggravated?" She could not answer, only gazed at me silently. Her voice had choked by then.

I immediately called the doctor at that hour of the night.

The doctor could not guess anything at first. Later he asked, "Has that pain increased? Why don't we administer the massage oil?" Saying this he picked up the bottle to find it empty.

He then asked my wife, "Have you taken this medicine by mistake?" My wife shook her head to quietly answer, "Yes".

The doctor immediately drove to his house to get the pump. I fell faintingly on my wife's bed.

Then she drew my head towards her chest like a mother trying to pacify her pained baby and with her two hands tried to touch and tell me what was going on in her mind. Only through that sad touch she spoke to me again and again, "Do not grieve. This has all worked out for the good. You will be happy, and I shall die happily thinking of your happiness."

When the doctor returned, my wife had been relieved of all suffering and pain associated with life.

Dakshinacharan drank water once more and said, "Oh! It is too warm!" Saying this, he quickly went out and strolled up and down quite a few times on the verandah. I could well sense that, though he did not want to say it, I was somehow magically drawing out words from him. He began to speak.

I married Manorama and returned back home. Manorama married me with her father's consent. But when I tried to speak words of caress or try to win her over with lines of love, she would not smile, she would be very serious. What doubt had struck her at which part of her heart, how was I to know?

At this juncture my addiction to drinking grew considerably.

Once in an autumn evening I was roaming with Manorama in our garden in Baranagore. It was eerily dark all around. One could not even hear the flapping of wings from the birds' nests. Only the heavily shaded pine trees on both sides of the path were shaking in the breeze, emitting a heavy noise.

Manorama wearily stretched herself on the white marble platform around that *bakul* tree, cradling her head between her arms. I too came and sat beside her.

There the darkness was intensified. Wherever the sky could be seen, was covered with stars. The droning of crickets from the bases of trees seemed to knit a thin line of sound up in the verge of a silence exiled from the vast expanse of the eternal sky.

I had drunk that evening. My mind was in an inebriated state. When my eyes adjusted to the darkness, the lightly etched out silhouette of the weary, unmindful woman painted in the pale hues of the shady forests seemed to create an inevitable emotion in me. I felt that she was a shadow and I would never succeed in embracing her totally. At that instant the peaks of the pine trees seemed to be set aflame, very slowly the waning yellow new moon seemed to perch upon the sky above the trees. The white moonlight fell on the face of the wearily-laid, white-*saried* woman on the white marble. I could stay no longer. Coming nearer, I took her hand in mine and said, "Manorama, you do not believe me, but I love you. I will never forget you."

As soon as I said these words, I startled. I remembered I had said those very words on some other day to someone else. And at that very moment from up above the heads of pine trees, over the branches of the *bakul* tree, lower than the yellow half-moon from the eastern end of the Ganges to its farthest western end a stream of loud laughter sounding *haha, haha, haha* flew across speedily. That was heart-piercing laughter or earth-piercing wailing, I cannot say for at that moment I fainted and fell down from the stone platform.

When I regained consciousness, I saw I was lying on my bed. My wife asked, "What happened to you suddenly?"

I trembled a little and said, "Didn't you hear how the skies around seemed to fill with the sound of a loud laughter?" My wife smiled, "Was that laughter? A long queue of birds were flying in a line—I could hear the flapping of their wings. Do you feel afraid at so little?"

The next morning I could feel that truly it had been the sound of birds flying across—wild ducks had migrated in this season from the North to the banks of the river. But as evening fell, I could believe in that no more. I would feel that all around the darkness, deepest laughter had been stored and, on the slightest pretext, would pierce that darkness and echo everywhere about me. It so happened that after evening I would not dare to utter a single word to Manorama.

Then I left our Baranagore residence and set sailing with Manorama in our boat. All my fears and apprehensions disappeared in the cool December breeze flowing across the river. I was very happy those few days. It seemed Manorama too was beguiled by the beauty around and had slowly begun to open the closed doors of her heart.

After passing the Ganges and the Khar at last we reached the Padma* river. The terrible Padma was then like the holed-up female serpent of the winter lying shrunk and lifeless, immersed in its long, never ending winter sleep. On the northern border lay the long stretched sand banks, desolate and bare, and the village mango groves on the upper banks on the south shivering with folded hands near the ferocious mouth of this demoness river. The Padma was tossing and turning in its slumber and the weakened land slopes on either side were collapsing loudly, one by one.

I found this spot convenient to anchor our boat and wander around.

One day both of us wandered far ahead on a stroll. As soon as the golden aura of the sunset disappeared, the clear moonlight of the full moon seemed to bloom

---

* a river in East Bengal now in Bangladesh, known for its fierce nature, prone to terrible floods

slowly all around. When the limitless, uncontrollable, resounding moonlight seemed to stretch over that unending, white sand bank almost reaching the horizon, it seemed that in this lovely, eternal dream world created by the magical full moon, we were the only two people existing and wandering about.

A red shawl had covered Manorama's head and framed her face, and also fully draped her entire body. When the silence deepened, and when there was nothing except unlimited, aimless whiteness and emptiness, Manorama very slowly took out her hand and caught hold of mine lightly. She appeared to come closer as if she wanted to hand over herself both in body and spirit, giving her life and youth to me in complete dependence. I thought with a heaving heart full of pleasure, can one love so freely inside one's room? You need this kind of bare, unlimited, eternal atmosphere to suit two young lovers. Then I felt, we had no home, no restrictions, nowhere to return; we could move hand in hand on this nomadic, aimless journey through this moonlit barrenness moving eternally in this unrestricted manner.

After walking for sometime we reached a place to find that in that sand expanse there appeared to be a pool of water in the centre—some water had been stored in that place after the Padma river had shifted away.

Upon that still, motionless, sleepy pool of water a long sketch of moonlight seemed to draw a faint line. We came to that spot and stood. Manorama in a moment of quiet introspection looked up at me. And the shawl slipped from her head. I lifted her moonlit, glowing face and kissed her.

At that moment amidst the desolate, lonely desert—someone cried out in solemn tone—"Who is she? Who is she? Who is she?"

I startled, my wife too shivered. But we soon understood that this was not a human voice, neither was it supernatural—only the call of the night birds roaming the river banks. They had been startled by the advent of so many people into their safe, solitary haven in the late hours of night.

Greatly disturbed by this fearful incident, both of us returned early to our boat. Manorama was tired, she slept almost as soon as we touched the bed. I was awake—in the dark there was someone standing near my bed where my mosquito net hung pointing out a single, long, shrunk, bony finger at the sleeping Manorama and whispering soft inaudible words in my ears and asking almost in refrain—"Who is she? Who is she? Who is she, my dear?"

I got up very fast and lit the lamp striking the matchstick. At that moment the shadowy figure disappeared. And a terrifying 'Ha Ha-haha-haha' sounding loud laughter shook my bed, my mosquito net and the entire boat freezing the blood of my perspiring body at an instant and flew out through the deep, dark night. With the Padma river flowing and the banks of the Padma passing by—that fierce laughter from time to eternity crossing the limits of men and countries and going further and further—slowly growing fainter and fainter. It seemed to cross the land of birth and death, slowly it seemed to be more shrill than the pointed end of a needle; I had never heard such a faint tone and could never have imagined it. I felt as if I was carrying the eternal sky on my head and though the sound travelled, it could never cross the boundaries of my brain. Soon all this became unbearable and I thought, I would never be able to sleep till I put the lights off. As I put off the lights to lie again, suddenly at that moment near my mosquito net, near my bed and in my ears the same muted voice began to cry in the darkness, "Who is she, who is she, who is she, my dear?" Synchronised with that in a similar rhythm there seemed to ring in my heart those very same words, "Who is she, who is she, who is she, my dear? Who is she, who is she, my dear?" The circular clock too seemed to come alive as it spread its arrows towards Manorama in that deep dark night in the silent boat and struck its rhythmical chords upon the shelf saying, "Who is she, who is she, who is she, my dear? Who is she, who is she, who is she, Who is she, dear?"

So saying, Dakshinacharan turned pale, and his voice seemed to choke. I touched him and said, "Have some water." At that moment the flame of the kerosene lamp flickered a few times and went off. Suddenly, I saw that it was daylight all around. The crows cawed. The birds chirped. A buffalo cart went screeching on the road facing my house. Dakshincharan's facial expressions seemed to transform dramatically. There remained no traces of any sort of fear. He appeared to be immensely cross with me and ashamed of himself for relating such intimate details to me, lost in the illusions created by the night and those imaginary fears and apprehensions born out of his drowsy consciousness. Without a word of greeting he suddenly got up and walked away as fast as he could.

The very same day at about midnight there was a knock again on my door, "Doctor! Doctor!"

✭✭✭✭✭

Four

Lost Jewels
Manihara

My boat was anchored at the side of that worn-out cemented river *ghat*.* The sun had set by then. The Muslim boatman was chanting his prayers on the roof of the boat. His silent prayers were being painted like portraits every fleeting moment on the canvas of the flaming sky of the western horizon. Innumerable, unaccountable array of colours falling on the statuesque, still waters of the river were gradually transforming from lighter to darker hues, from golden to rust and from one colour to another.

Sitting alone on the *peepal*-rooted stone embankment facing the huge dilapidated, broken windowed palatial house with the hanging, supportless balconies on this evening of droning crickets, my dry eyes were about to water when suddenly, startling me from top to toe, a voice said, "Sir, where do you hail from?"

I looked at him. He was thin from malnutrition and appeared rather neglected by Lady Luck. His appearance was similar to that of most of the people working under the British government in Bangladesh—as unkempt as they were.

He had worn a dirty, oily, open-bottomed short coat made of Assamese *matka*† cloth over a *dhoti*‡ and

---
* river embankment
† a type of material generally found in eastern India
‡ a cotton cloth tied around the waist

appeared to have just returned from work. And when he should have been eating some snacks, this unfortunate man had come to the river shore only to enjoy the evening breeze.

The stranger took a seat beside the stone steps. I said, "I am coming from Ranchi."

"What do you do?"

"I am in business."

"What is it?"

"Silkworm and wool."

"What is your name?"

I stopped a while and uttered a name. But that was not my real name.

The gentleman was not satisfied. He asked again, "What have you come here for?"

I said, "Change of weather."

The man was a bit surprised, "Sir, for about six years I have enjoyed this weather and on an average I have been taking fifteen grains of quinine along with it, but till now I have not received any wondrous results."

I said, "But you must admit that here there would be a considerable change in atmosphere from Ranchi."

He said, "Yes sir, without any doubt. Where would you live here?"

I showed him the dilapidated house along the embankment and said, "This house."

Perhaps the man suspected that I had come to this ruined house in search of some hidden treasure. But he did not argue further on this topic, he only went on to narrate in detail that incident which had happened in this accursed house fifteen years back.

The man was the schoolmaster here. A pair of large eyes underneath his pate was burning with an unnatural intensity from within the depths of his hunger-struck and sickly face. Seeing him, I was reminded of the English poet Coleridge's creation, the Ancient Mariner.

The boatman had finished praying and had concentrated on cooking. The last hues of the setting sun slowly disappeared and the desolate, dark house on the shores stood fixed in itself like a huge ghost—still and quiet. The schoolmaster began.

* * * *

About ten years back, before I arrived in this village Phanibhushan Saha lived in this house. He had inherited his childless paternal uncle Shri Durgamohan Saha's huge property and business.

But this person was bugged by 'modernity.' He had studied quite a bit. He would walk with shoes on to visit foreign offices and speak strictly in correct English. And, on top of that, he had kept a beard, thus he didn't stand a chance of achieving a promotion from any British employer. He looked like a typical Bengali of the new era at the first sight.

He had created further trouble even at home. His wife was college-educated and also beautiful. Thus, there were no traces of old traditions left. So much so that the assistant surgeon would be called in cases of illness. External appearance, dress and jewellery too seemed to grow in stature hand in hand with such a modern attitude.

I think, Sir, you are married, hence it would be unnecessary to tell you that the female race loves raw mangoes, hot chillies and a stern husband. The unfortunate man who is deprived of the love of his wife need not be ugly or poor—he just has to be timid.

If you ask me why this is so, I can answer you in as many ways as I can think. When one can never practise what one is suited for or is instinctively gifted for, he or she can never be totally fulfilled—just as the deer which chooses the firm trunk of a tree to sharpen its horn does not achieve satisfaction from rubbing its horn on the soft trunk of a banana tree. From eternity whenever a distinction has been made between men and women, women have practised the art of tempting and possessing difficult men through several tactics. The poor woman whose husband surrenders himself without any effort on her part feels that she is totally rendered useless—the art of capturing hearts learnt through centuries from the time-tested ways of great grandmothers, the fiery glances, tearful eyes and snaky embraces then seem to be in vain.

A woman seeks to ensnare a man and thereby claim his love, but when the husband is too simple and does not give her reason to do so the husband is doomed, and the wife more so.

Men initiated by the customs of the new era have lost their natural God-given noble, yet barbaric, instincts and thus have made modern conjugal affairs rather light and casual. The unfortunate Phanibhushan had come out of the confines of modern education quite simple and liberal, hence, he could not do well in business, neither was he lucky in love.

Phanibhushan's wife Manimalika received all his love without any effort on her part. She got the typical *dhakai** sarees of Dacca to wear without shedding tears and without severe tantrums; she even received beautiful ornaments like the beautiful *bajubandh*.† In this

---

* typical, hand-woven sarees of Dacca
† a beautiful bracelet worn on the upper arm

way, her natural feminity and, along with it, her love had remained static. She would only 'take', never 'give' in return. Her timid and foolish husband would think that carrying on 'giving' was the only way to 'receive' in return. He had thought quite the contrary, that is.

The consequence of all came to be that she would consider her husband a machine who could produce *dhakai* sarees and ornaments for her; and this machine was so efficient that there had never been any need to lubricate its wheels.

Phanibhushan's birthplace was Phulbere, and business here. He had to stay most of his time here on account of work. His mother did not live in Phulbere, but his aunts and several others lived there. But Phanibhushan had not wedded a beautiful wife for the sake of others. Hence he isolated his wife from the rest of the world and kept her near him in this mansion. But a basic difference between the right to keep a wife and any other right was that it did not mean that, if you isolate your wife from others and keep her to yourself, you are always assured of her heart and her company all the time and all the way.

His wife did not speak much, there was no communication between her neighbours and herself. She never took the opportunity of any religious ritual to feed a Brahmin or two; neither did she bother to give alms to a poor Vaishnavite sage-woman. She did not waste anything, she would save whatever she received except, perhaps, the caresses of her husband. The strangest matter was that she had not allowed even a bit of her youthful beauty to wane. As a result, people say, she appeared as fresh and young as a fourteen-year-old when she was about twenty-four. Perhaps the ones whose hearts are like icebergs—those who have never experienced the pangs and sufferings of love—remain young and fresh for a long period. Perhaps they can preserve their interior and exterior beings almost like a miser guards his assets.

Manimalika blossomed like a densely leaved, extremely green and fresh creeper; but God ordained to keep her childless like a fruitless plant. He never bestowed on her that very gift which she would understand better than the jewels in her iron chest, that which could melt the iceberg in her heart like the newly born sun on a fresh spring morning through its soft and delicate warmth, thus transforming it into a spring of love and affection showering into itself the bare world all around her.

But Manimalika was very efficient in her household matters. She never kept more servants than necessary. She could not bear to think that someone else would take a salary for a job which she herself could complete. She never thought of anyone else, she never loved anyone else, she would only work and save a lot of money. Hence she never suffered from grief, remorse or illness. She would live in an impenetrable world of good health, undisturbed contentment and accumulated wealth and prosperity, feeling strong and secure.

This would have been sufficient for most husbands—not only sufficient, it would have been invaluable for most. We do not feel that we have a waistline till we feel a sharp pain at the spot. Similarly, when we suffer the pangs of love, we realise day in and day out that there is a woman in the household—and this is called the 'waist ache' of a household. Extreme subjugation and devotion towards a husband might be a matter of pride for a woman, but is of no comfort to a husband.

Is it the duty of a man to constantly measure how much of his wife's love he has been lucky to receive and how much of it has been held back? I do my duties, and let my wife go about her own—broadly this is how a home functions. How much has been spelt out without word, what are the feelings expressed, how many secret indications lie dormant inside verbal clarity, each single molecule and atom signifying how much of greatness discerning such minute power of what is love and what is not, have never come easily to a 'man'—perhaps God has never gifted to him nor has felt the need to do so.

It is the prerogative of women to weigh the pros and cons of the scales of a man's love. They probe deeply into the minds of men to find what lies concealed in their words and find out the real meaning of their words from their behaviour, gauging them narrowly and examining every particle, since a man's love is for them their strength, the profound investment of their business of life.

But what the Lord has denied them, recently men have acquired that power. The poets have defied the ordains of the Lord and gifted this powerful instrument, this all-perceiving, painful yardstick without hesitation to all humans. I do not blame the Lord. He had created men and women different from each other, but that difference is slowly disappearing with the advent of modernisation. Now, women are turning more into men, and men into women, thus peace and discipline have bid goodbye to our homes. Now, before getting married, the bride and bridegroom, seemingly unable to decide whether they are marrying a man or woman, await their fate with trembling, apprehensive hearts.

Are you annoyed? Well, I live alone, banished from my wife. Many deep thoughts regarding home and household appear to me from afar—and these are not to be related to the students—I just spelt them out to you as a point of discussion. Do ponder on them.

The crux of the whole matter was that though there was no flaw in her cookery skills and the *paan** which she dressed were never fraught with excessive limestone, Phanibhushan's heart was always troubled by some unknown pain. His wife was an epitome of perfection— she had no faults or blemishes—but her husband, nevertheless, was not happy. He would aim at capturing the hollow depths of the heart of his better half by constantly gifting her diamonds and pearls, but they would land up only in the iron chest, and never find a place in her heart. His uncle Durgamohan did not feel the fine nuances of love, and would never ask for it as thirstily as he did and never showered it as much as he did, but would receive it in abundance from his aunt. You cannot be a businessman if you are a liberal modernist, and to be a husband you must be like a 'man'—have no doubts about it.

At that moment jackals from the surrounding shrubs cried out at a very high pitch. The schoolmaster's narrative flow was slightly disturbed. It appeared as if, in that dark meeting hall those amorous jackals were roaring in amused laughter at the schoolmaster's description of conjugal bliss or at the attitude of Phanibhushan—muscularity weakened by liberal thinking.

After their emotional outburst subsided, and the atmosphere appeared doubly calm, the master rolled his huge bright eyes in the darkness of the evening and began his story once again.

---

* betel leaves dressed with betel-nut and other ingredients usually eaten after meals in India, good for digestion

Suddenly there appeared to be a problem in Phanibhushan's complicated and widespread business. A non-businessman like me would not be able to fathom and explain exactly what it was. The fact was, that suddenly for some reason he was finding it difficult to sustain credibility in the market. If only for about five days he could arrange for one-and-a-half lakh rupees, and could display it fleetingly in the market, in a moment he would overcome this problem and his business could run smoothly once again.

But he could not organise the required sum. He could not ask the local moneylenders for fear that his business would be further negatively affected if there was a rumour that he had resorted to taking loans for survival. Hence he had to look for unknown lenders for the loan, where he would have to pawn suitable assets against it. If one could pawn jewellery the job would be much simpler and faster as that did not involve legal complications.

Phanibhushan went to meet his wife. He did not have the courage to meet his own wife as naturally as a husband does. Unfortunately, he loved his wife as the hero of a romantic epic loves the heroine, where one has to tread softly in love and can not speak aloud all that one feels—that love whose terrible attraction like the attraction between the sun and the earth keeps a great distance between each other.

Nevertheless, in some situations, even the hero of poetry has been compelled to broach the topics of bonds and handbills and promissory notes; but the tone has been obstructed, sentences have remained unfinished, and there has remained a confusion of emotions and painful deliberation even in the clearest of practicalities. The unfortunate Phanibhushan could not clearly spell out "My love, I am in dire need, would you give me your jewellery?"

He tried to say the same to her, but very meekly. When Manimalika turned a stern face and answered neither yes nor no, he received a cruel blow but did not retort. He did not possess a trace of the supposedly 'masculine' aggressiveness. Where he should have taken away through coercion, he even suppressed his innermost feelings. He felt that no matter what happened, he would never allow 'might' to take over from the 'right' of love, which was supreme for him. If one rebuked him on this, he would probably argue in his most refined manner and say, 'If I have lost credit in the financial market, let us suppose unjustifiably, even then I have no right to plunder the market. Similarly, if my wife does not trust me and does not hand over her jewellery to me willingly, I can never snatch if from her through force. Credit in the market is like 'love' at home, sheer physical force is only used in battlefield.' Had the Lord created man so vastly generous, so strong and so large only to judge and measure finer points of debates at every step? Does he have the leisure to rest and feel such extremely delicate feelings with such infinite platitude? Does that suit his style?

Whatever it was, proud in his own elevated thoughts, Phanibhushan travelled to Calcutta for other means of managing the amount without even touching the jewellery of his wife.

Generally, in worldly life, a wife knows her husband much more than a husband knows her; but, if the nature of a husband's character is too refined, the entire picture is not always projected in the microscopic view of his wife. Phanibhusan's wife did not quite comprehend Phanibhusan. The efficiency of an ordinary woman's understanding is the built-up of certain unrefined, primitive ideals born out of centuries of ignorance. The newly-born liberalist men are distinctly 'out' of this category. They are a class apart. They are turning out to be as mysterious as women. They cannot be placed within the usual broad categories enlisted for men as barbaric, foolish, unfeeling or blind to emotions. Hence Manimalika beckoned her minister for advice. A far-related brother of hers hailing from her village was working under the manager of Phanibhushan's estate. He did not possess the efficiency to gain a raise, thus he would try to gain some salary by virtue of his relationship with Manimalika and also manage some other perks.

Manimalika called him and related her woes and asked him, "Now what do you advise?"

He shook his head wisely as if to say that all was not hunky-dory. He said, "Babu will never succeed in arranging the full amount, he is bound to ask for your jewellery at the end of the day."

As far as she understood human beings, Manimalika too felt that this was a strong possibility, and justifiably so. Her worries grew further. She was deprived of any offspring; she had a husband but did not feel his presence in her heart. Thus whatever she possessed, what was dear to her heart, what was *growing* every day like her child— that which was not a fairy tale but tested gold, that which was a jewel adorning the neck, the chest, or the head and forehead, the treasured belongings of long years—to think that all of that would be thrown into the deepest pits of business in a moment made her blood curdle. She asked, "What coan be done?"

Madhusudan said, "Collect your ornaments and hurry to your father's home." The sly Madhusudan thought of a plan whereby he could appropriate a share of those ornaments, in fact majority of them. Manimalika immediately agreed to this proposal.

Towards the end of the *Ashaad*,* the monsoon month, one evening a boat anchored itself in this embankment by the river. On a densely clouded, deeply dark hours at dawn amidst the sleepless croaking of frogs, Manimalika covered with a heavy shawl from top to toe, stepped into the boat. Madhusudan woke up from inside the boat and said, "Give the jewellery box to me." Mani said, "I'll give later, now untie the boat."

The boat was untied and it sailed away in the swift currents of water. Over the night, Manimalika had worn all her ornaments one by one till there was no space uncovered from top to toe. She had the fear that the jewellery could be misplaced if she carried it in a box. But once she had worn those ornaments, no one would succeed in looting them until and unless she was murdered. Seeing no box with her, Madhusudan could not guess anything; he could not have imagined that underneath the heavy shawl lay concealed Manimalika's body and soul along with the ornaments which she cared for even more than her body and soul! Manimalika could not understand Phanibhushan, but did not fail to comprehend Madhusudan. Madhusudan had left a letter with the manager that he was going to reach the mistress to her father's home. The manager who was working with the family since the time of Phanibhushan's father was quite annoyed and wrote to his master. Though the letter was written in poor

---
* a monsoon month in the Bengali calendar

language and was full of errors, he made his disapproval quite evident saying that it was not masculine enough to unquestioningly support the wrong actions of a wife.

Phanibhushan well understood what was working in Manimalika's mind. He was hurt by the terrible thought, 'I am trying my best to collect money through other means, not asking for the ornaments of my wife even in this hour of acute loss; but she still suspects me. She does not recognise me even today.'

He should have been terribly angered at this severe injustice done to him, but Phanibhushan was only a little hurt. A man acts as the carrier of the justice of the Lord, He has ignited the fire of thunder in him. But if a man fails to light up this fire of anger in himself whenever he or anyone else faces a conflict of justice, then shame on him! A man's fury should burn like a fire at the least cause, and a woman weep like the clouds on a *Shravan** sky without any cause—perhaps the Lord had ordained as such, but this theory does not seem to hold true any longer.

Phanibhushan addressed his blundering wife spoke to himself, "If this is your justice, then let it be so, I will carry on with my duty." Phanibhushan should have been born five or more centuries later when the world would be ruled only by spiritual power. But this futuristic Phanibhushan was unfortunately born in the nineteenth century and had married a woman of the pre-medieval times—a woman whose kind of intelligence has been described as 'destructive' in the scriptures. Phanibhushan never wrote a line to his wife and promised himself that he would never utter a word on this matter to her. What a strange punishment!

---

* monsoon month in the Bengali calendar following Ashaad

After ten days a relieved Phanibhushan returned home. He had been able to collect a considerable sum of money to get out of his immediate predicament. He knew that by now Manimalika would have returned home after depositing all her jewellery at her father's place. Thinking of how Manimalika would be ashamed of herself and regret her hasty, unnecessary step when he presented himself as a man, successful in his endeavour in place of the lowly figure asking for alms as he had appeared to her earlier, Phanibhushan reached the door of their private bed chamber situated in the interior of the house.

He found the door shut. He broke the lock to enter and found the room deserted. The iron chest lay in the corner—there was no trace of the ornaments.

His heart missed a beat. He felt this world was aimless and *love* and trade or business a futile exercise. We are giving our lifeblood for every rod of this cage-like world, but there lives no bird inside; it escapes even when it is kept therein. Phanibhushan kicked away this empty worldly cage wound around such involvement which stretched beyond eternity from his heart and soul and threw it far beyond.

Phanibhushan did not want to try searching for his wife. He thought if she wished, she would come back. The old Brahmin manager came and advised, 'How can we keep quiet; We have to find out about the mistress'. So saying, he sent someone to her father's place to find out. News came back—neither Manimalika nor Madhusudan had reached there so far.

Then search began everywhere. Men ran around enquiring at every embankment along the riverside. The police was informed to search for Madhusudan—no one could give any information on which was the boat, who was the boatman, which path they had followed and where they had gone.

Giving up all hopes of her return, one evening Phanibhushan entered his discarded bed chamber. The day was *Janmastami*,* Lord Krishna's birthday, and it was raining incessantly from the morning. Every year on this festival a fair would be held at the end of the village. A *jatra* for the general public had just begun on the open stage built there. The tune of the song played in the *jatra* seemed to be very faint amidst the sound of the heavy incessant rain outside. Where the loose-hinged door lay hanging over the window, Phanibhushan sat alone in the darkness—totally unaware of the monsoon breeze, splatter of rain and the song of the *jatra* floating into the room. An art-studio-composed pair of photographs of Goddesses Lakshmi and Saraswati hung from the wall, a *gamcha*† and a towel on the clothes rack as well as a thin-bordered and narrow striped sari, wrung around, pleated and ready to wear. In the corner of the room, lay a copper box on the teapot, which still carried a few withered *paans* which Manimalika had herself prepared. The glass sideboard contained so many relics of hers—dolls of china clay preserved from childhood, bottles of essence, coloured glass decanters, fashionable cards, seashells and some soap boxes with nothing in them carefully decorated and organised on the shelves.

Even the tiny circular favourite kerosene lamp of hers which she would prepare and light herself and keep on the case was standing in the same position, extinguished and pale. Only this tiny lamp was the silent witness to Manimalika's last few moments in the

---

* Lord Krishna's birthday celebrated by Hindus in India
† a typical material used for drying bodies

bed chamber; to think that for one who leaves such a feeling of loneliness, could leave so many signatures of affection and care of a living heart on inanimate objects, traces of an identity, so many histories and so much behind herself! 'Come Manimalika, come, light your lamp, light up your chamber, stand before the mirror and wear the saree you have pleated with such care! Only your presence, your eternal youth, your unperishable beauty could awaken these scattered numerous, orphaned inanimate beings to life; the silent tears of these dumb, lifeless objects have converted this home into a graveyard.'

No one knew when in the dead of night the rainfall and the *jatra* song had ceased. Phanibhushan sat near the window as before. There was such an all-encompassing, unpenetrable darkness beyond the open window that he felt it was the heavily dark gateway to heaven, and if he could stand and cry for something lost forever, it would appear perhaps even for a fleeting moment. Perhaps the lost golden past could draw a line on the blackness of the portrait of death—on this doubly hardened stony black wall ahead!

Just then, along with a loud noise, the heavy clanging of ornaments could be heard from somewhere afar. It almost seemed as if the sound was travelling from the *ghat* of the river. Thrilled to the core, Phanibhushan tried hard to push and penetrate the severe darkness with his two anxious eyes to see beyond. His joyous heart and eager eyes ached but he could not see anything. As he strived to catch a glimpse, the darkness seemed to intensify, the world appeared more and more shadowy and mysterious. It seemed as if Nature, startled by the sudden arrival of an intruder at the dead of night trying to peep through the window to see its secret valley of death, had hurriedly pulled the dark curtains a little more.

Gradually, the sound seemed to cross the topmost steps of the river *ghat*, and move towards the mansion and ceased when face to face with it. The guard had locked the gates and gone to enjoy the *jatra*. It was then that on that shut main gate, the sound of a hard object beating against the wood along with the clanging of ornaments seemed to create a strange cacophony as if someone was knocking against the door pleading to be let in. Phanibhushan could wait no longer. He rose up, crossed the chambers whose lamps had long been extinguished, descended the dark staircase, came near the main door to find it shut. The door was locked from outside. Phanibhushan struggled to push the door with his two hands. Suddenly the tussle and its noise seemed to wake him up from his stupor with a start. He found that he had descended to the ground floor in his state of slumber. He was drenched in perspiration, hands and feet as cold as ice, and his heart was beating like the flickering flames of a burning lamp about to go off. He woke from his trance only to see that there was no sound any more outside, only the seasonal showers were still falling in rhythm and singers of the *jatra* were singing tunes of early daybreak.

Although the entire event was a dream, it was so close to his heart and reality that Phanibhushan felt as if he had been deprived of achieving his impossible desired ideal only by a few seconds. The tune of the classical *raga* of early mornings, *bhairavi*,* from far away mingled with the sound of rainfall contrived to speak to him saying—this awakening is a dream, the world an illusion.

---

* a special raga or tune of Indian classical music sung in early mornings

There was *jatra* the next day too and the guard was on leave. Phanibhushan issued orders that the front door should be kept open overnight. The guard said, "So many people are coming from different corners of the country to see this fair, it would not be safe to keep the door ajar." But Phanibhushan did not agree. The guard said, "Then I have to be on duty tonight". Phanibhushan said, "No, nothing of the sort, you must go to the *jatra*." The guard was astonished.

The next evening Phanibhushan extinguished the lamp and sat near the window of his bed chamber once more. There were dense monsoon clouds all around and an atmosphere of uncertain stillness prevailed as if it was waiting for something to happen. The incessant croaking of frogs and sound of loud chorus floating from the *jatra* did not disrupt that silence, but succeeded only in striking an incongruous chord of absurdity.

The frogs and crickets, even the singers in the *jatra* group ceased their chatter at a very late hour and the veil of darkness of another kind seemed to fall upon the darkness of night. He could sense that the time had arrived.

As the night before, a similar kind of thumping and clanging noise seemed to arise from the river *ghat*. But Phanibhushan turned his eyes away. He feared lest all his desires, all his efforts fail because of his own eager anxiety and impatience. So that his senses were not overpowered by the intensity of his emotions, he tried to apply all his efforts to control his mind, and sat as fixed as a wooden statue.

The jingle of ornaments today seemed to rise gradually, slowly, from the *ghat* and enter the wide open front door. He could hear the sound moving in circular motions all along the circular staircase inside the mansion, slowly ascending. Phanibhushan was struggling to keep himself under control, his heart was tossing and turning like a tiny boat on a storm-tossed ocean and he almost lost his breath. The sound gradually ascended the circular staircase and, crossing the balcony, seemed to come closer to his room. Ultimately, the clattering and clanging seemed to cease at the doorstep of his bed chamber. Now it only had to cross the doorstep.

Phanibhushan could stay no longer. All his pent-up emotions arose in an overflowing rush; he moved up from the seat in lighting speed and cried aloud, "Moni!". At the same moment he was startled from his stupor to see that even the window-panes were echoing and pulsating with the cry of his anxious heart. There were the usual noise and weary voices singing in the *jatra* and the chorus of the frogs in the background.

Phanibhushan beat his forehead hard with his fist.

The fair was over the next day. The shopkeepers and the *jatra* group had left. Phanibhushan sent orders that after evening there should be no one besides himself in that mansion. The servants decided that the master was engaged in some kind of tantric rites. Phanibhushan fasted the entire day.

Phanibhushan sat facing the window in the evening when the house had been deserted. There were no scattered clouds that day, and the stars looked extremely bright in the clear and clean sky. The waning moon would take a long while to arrive on the scene. As the fair had ended, there were absolutely no boats on the full river and the village, tired of keeping awake for two consecutive ceremonial nights, was immersed in deep slumber.

Phanibhushan was sitting on a bench and gazing at the stars while resting his head on the back of the bench, looking up. He was thinking that when he was nineteen and studying in a college in Calcutta, he would lie upon the grass in the circular square at evening time resting his head upon his arm and gaze at those stars of eternity and would remember his in-laws' house beside the river shores and a secluded room in that house where lived a fourteen-year-old, adolescent Moni with her bright, youthful features. The separation of those days was so sweet. How the pulsating lights of those stars could synchronise with the beatings of youthful hearts and play a curious melody of spring time every now and then! Today, those same stars had lit up their flames on the sky as if proclaiming Mahmudgar's poetic words which said, "This world is exceedingly strange!"

One by one, the stars slowly vanished. A darkness descended from the heavens and a darkness rose from the world, and both united as if they were the upper and lower eyelashes of one eye. Today, Phanibhushan was at peace with himself. He knew for sure that today he would succeed in his goal, and death would unveil its mystery to its worshipper.

Similar to the night before, that sound ascended the steps of the *ghat* from within the waters of the river. Phanibhushan sat with a still, determined heart, with eyes shut as if he was meditating. The sound entered inside the court through the unguarded front gate, it travelled up and down the circular staircase inside desolate interiors of the mansion, crossed the long corridor and stopped for a moment at the door of the bed chamber.

Phanibhushan's heart grew anxious, and his hair stood up; but he did not open his eyes. The sound crossed the doorstep and entered the dark room. It stopped at the clothes rack where the saree was pleated and kept, at the tin case where the kerosene lamp stood, at the teapot where the prepared betal lay withered in its chest, near the side-board full of curios and at last came very close to Phanibhushan and stopped.

Then Phanibhushan opened his eyes and saw, the light of the just risen moon had entered the room, and a skeleton stood right in front of his bench. The skeleton wore eight rings in eight fingers, *chakra*-like ornaments on the palms, lower arms adorned with thick gold bangles, forearms with *bajuband*, necklace on her neck; a thin line of gold on her hair parting and each bone on that figure was adorned with gold and diamond jewellery—dazzling and glowing. The ornaments seemed to be loosely dangling but never falling off that bony structure. What was most terrifying was that, in that bone-structured face, the two eyes were lifelike; the same black eyeballs, those long and black eyelashes, that dewy brightness, the same unshaken, still and calm glance. Phanibhushan saw the same two eyes at this midnight hour of this *Shravan* day in clear moonlight what he had first set his eyes upon eighteen years back one day in a brightly lit wedding hall amidst the orchestra playing the *shahana raag*; two well-shaped, beautiful, jet black, expressive eyes had met his during the *Shubho drishti**wedding ritual when the bride and the groom look at each other for the first time and their eyes meet. On seeing them, his blood curled up in fear. He tried hard to shut his eyes once more but could not; his eyes kept staring fixedly like a dead man's eyes.

The skeleton keeping its eyes fixed on the face of dumbstruck Phanibhushan, lifted up her right hand and beckoned him silently signalling by the fingers. The

---

* a Bengali wedding ritual where the bride and the bridegroom look at each other for the first time and their eyes meet

diamond rings on the bones of the four fingers shone brilliantly.

Phanibhushan stood up, spellbound. The skeleton moved towards the door; the ornaments and bones made a heavy metallic sound as they hit against each other. Phanibhushan followed it like a hypnotised dummy. It crossed the balcony, descended the deeply dark, circular staircase round and round making the peculiar, clanging, clattering and beating noise and ultimately touching the ground floor. It crossed the verandah downstairs and entered the lampless deserted court. At last it crossed the court and went out to the garden path covered with pebbles. The pebbles made a strange noise when the bony feet trampled on them. Where the faint moonlight had lost its way somewhere amidst the dense forests, there in that rain drenched, densely dark, shadowy path through the rows of glow-worms, both of them walked on till they reached the *ghat* of the river.

The bejewelled skeleton slowly and steadily, without any hesitation, descended the stone steps making a hard sound—the same steps from which the sound had risen in the first place. A long stretch of moonlight was shining brightly on the forceful currents of water of the river full to the brim after monsoon.

The skeleton went down into the river. Following it, Phanibhushan too stepped into the water. As soon as he touched the water, Phanibhushan woke up from the trance. There was no guide before him any more, only the trees stood on the banks of the river—still and silent and the moon above them was quiet, looking at them with a glint of surprise. Shivering violently from top to toe, Phanibhushan lost control over his feet and fell into the strong currents of the river. Though he knew swimming his nerves were not under his control. He woke up from his trance only for a second, touched the shores of reality and, the next moment, was immersed in the utmost depths of slumber.

The schoolmaster ended his story and stopped for a while. As he stopped talking, it was felt that in the meantime, besides him, all the others of this world had been lost in an eerie silence. I did not speak for long and he could not observe my facial expressions either.

He asked me, "Didn't you believe this story?"

I asked, "Do you believe it?"

He said, "No. I can give you some reasons for my answer. Firstly, Lady Nature is not a novelist, she has plenty of work to do".

I said, "Secondly, Phanibhushan Saha is 'my' name." The schoolmaster, not the least ashamed said, "Then I did guess correctly. What was the name of your wife?"

I said, "Nrityakali."

Five

Metamorphosis
Samapti (Bengali)

I

Apurva Krishna is returning home from Calcutta after his graduation. The river is small. It quite dries up after the monsoon. Nowadays, after the advent of *Sravan*,* it has swelled up and is now moving, on almost touching the village fencing and the bamboo shoots.

Today the sun has appeared over the cloudless sky after a long and dreary monsoon. If we could see the picture which had been created in the mind of the young man seated in a boat, we could find out how the river of imagination generated therein had flooded to the brim with the onset of the monsoons and was now glittering brightly in the light and creating a gurgling sound.

The boat entered the embankment. One could see the terrace of Apurva's house appearing behind the trees from the bank of the river. No one was aware of the arrival of Apurva and hence there was none to receive him. Apurva joyfully descended on the steps hurriedly, carrying his own bag preventing the boatman from helping him.

As soon as he alighted—the bank was slippery and he fell on the wet clay ground, bag and baggage. As

*monsoon month of July-August in Bengali calendar

soon as he fell, suddenly from somewhere a very sweet, loud and clear wave of laughter came across and startled the birds sitting on the *peepul* tree nearby.

Apurva was extremely embarrassed but he quickly controlled himself and looked around. He saw heaps of new bricks from the merchant boats kept on the bank and there, on top of them, sat a young girl roaring with laughter as if her seams would burst open.

Apurva recognised the girl as the daughter of their new neighbour, Mrinmayi. They lived beside a distant big river but had to leave the place due to floods. They had settled here in this village for about two or three years.

One would hear a lot of unpleasant tales about this girl. The men would affectionately call her a 'mad' girl, but not the women of the village. They were always scared, anxious and worried about her reckless nature. She would play only with the boys of the village; and treat girls of her own age group with utmost indifference. This girl was considered a fearful figure in the children's circle.

She was powerful perhaps because she was the pampered daughter of her father. Though Mrinmayi's mother would always complain against her husband to her friends regarding this, she could never forget how much her husband loved his daughter and how he would be terribly hurt if he would see Mrinmayi's tears, and thus she could never say anything to her daughter which would hurt her.

Mrinmayi was dusky. Her short curly hair fell upon her shoulders. Her face exhibited a boyish expression. Her large black eyes reflected neither shame nor fear, nor any kind of a natural-feminine expression. Her figure was tall, healthy and strong. No one ever questioned whether she was still young or grown up, or else by now people would have criticised her parents for keeping her unmarried for so long. Whenever an unknown *zamindar's* boat anchored in the village river embankment the villagers would gear up in full form respectfully and the women present there would pull the veils over their faces almost to their nose tips like one pulls the curtain over an open stage. Suddenly Mrinmayi would appear running from somewhere with a naked child in her arms swaying her curly hair over her shoulders. She would stand there like a fearless baby deer stands in a land where there are no hunters, nor any kind of danger, and look around curiously. Then she would go back and tell the children of her own group all about this new creature's whereabouts in great detail.

Our Apurva had seen this uninhibited young woman a few times whenever he would come home for his holidays, and had even thought about her at leisure or even while at work. One chances to see quite a few faces but somehow there are only one or two which touch the inner crevices of the heart. That comes about not only for beauty, but for a certain other special quality. And that quality was, perhaps, transparency. Human nature does not manifest itself clearly in most faces, but a face which reveals that mysterious world hidden inside the dark caves of the mind may be noticed even amongst thousands and remains imprinted in the heart in a moment. An impatient, insolent feminity played upon the face of this girl all the time like a free and sprightly wild deer, and that was exactly why this lively face once seen could never be forgotten.

It would be futile to remind the readers that however sweet Mrinmayi's amused laughter might sound to others, it was slightly painful for the unfortunate Apurva. He submitted the bag hurriedly in the hands of the boatman and, red in the face, started walking in quick steps towards his house.

Nature's arrangement was pretty beautiful. The banks of the river, shade of the trees, song of the birds, the morning sunshine and twenty years of age—what more could one ask for? Though the heap of bricks was nothing romantic, the one who was sitting upon them had managed to create a pleasant picture even on those dry and hard pieces of stone. But oh! Cruel fate had conspired to transform all poetry into satire just with his first step into this pretty picture, thereby marring all its beauty.

II

Apurva reached home, his shawl and bag all soaked in mud, running away from those pile of bricks with the peals of laughter ringing in his ears, following the path shaded by tall trees.

His widowed mother was thrilled at his sudden arrival. At that very instance men ran far and near in search of thickened milk, curd, the *Rohu** fish and there arose quite a furore even amongst the neighbours in the locality.

After lunch, Apurva's mother broached the topic of his marriage. Apurva was prepared for that. The reason being there were plenty of proposals all along but the young man following new modern age dictates had obstinately declared that he would not marry till he

---

* a variety of freshwater fish cooked on special occasions in Bengal

graduated from college. Thus, his mother had been waiting patiently all these days. Now there was no way he could avoid it. So Apurva said, "Let me see the girl first, then we will decide." The mother said, "I have chosen the bride, you do not have to worry." But Apurva was worried about that very topic and so he said, "I cannot marry without seeing the girl." The mother thought she had never heard such a strange thing before, though she agreed.

That night after Apurva had put off the lamp and retired to bed the same open-hearted, high-pitched sweet laughter overpowered the same noises of the rainy night and travelled from far beyond all silence and reached his solitary, sleepless bed, ringing continuously in his ears. His heart began to hurt him, all the time telling him that he must recede the downfall of the morning in some way. The stupid young girl did not know that 'I' Apurva Krishna was highly qualified, and had spent a fairly long time in Calcutta; I was not any ordinary village boy who could be laughed at and ignored (just because suddenly I had slipped and fallen in the mud).

The next day Apurva was supposed to go and see the girl. She did not stay very far, she lived in the same locality. He dressed with special care. He changed from *dhoti* and shawl to a silk cloak, a rounded turban on the head, and wore his burnished pair of shoes, took his silk umbrella and set out in the morning.

There was great celebration once he reached his probable in-laws' residence. At last, the trembling girl was brought to the prospective groom at the right moment, all made-up and groomed with a silver strip tied around her bun dressed in a thin, colourful saree. She came in and kept sitting alone in the corner, quietly resting her face almost on her knees and a middle-aged maid stayed behind her just to offer moral support.

The bride's younger brother was intensely observing this stranger who was about to enter their family uncalled for—keenly examining this man's turban, watch chain and newly evolved beard. Apurva twirled his moustache for sometime and finally asked seriously, "What do you study?" He did not receive any reply from the well-covered bundle of shyness. However, being asked several times and thumped on the back encouragingly by the maid quite a few times, the girl ultimately replied with bated breath and mumbling words that she had read *Charupath** first book, the Grammar principles, first details of Geography, Algebra and the History of India. Suddenly, from nowhere a stormy noise was heard coming from the back and within a moment Mrinmayi entered the room running and panting aloud, swinging her long hair violently. She did not care to glance Apurva's way at all and straightaway began to tug at Rakhal's arm impatiently. All this time Rakhal was intensely busy practising his power of observation, and hence he refused to get up. The maid tried her very best to chide Mrinmayi forcefully, keeping control over the volume of her voice. Apurva Krishna sat, stillness personified, trying his best to call upon all the gravity and pride he could summon with his turbaned head and began pulling nervously at the watch chain on his coat. At long last when Mrinmayi found that she was not going to succeed in disturbing her companion, she slapped his back with a loud thump, then suddenly pulled out the veil of the bride and ran out of the room like a receding typhoon. The maid grumbled within herself and Rakhal began to chuckle

---

* textbook on Bengali alphabets

loudly at the sudden exposure of his sister from within the veil. As regards the terrible blow on his back he did not seem to think of it as an injustice, for such exchanges were going on within them almost all the time. So much so that when sometime back Mrinmayi's hair would fall upon her back much below her shoulders, it was Rakhal who had dared to come one day from the back and scissor her long hair. Mrinmayi had than snatched the scissors from him very angrily and noisily severed her remaining hair in an unkind manner. Her locks of curly hair lay on the floor like bunches of black grapes severed from the branches. Such was the code of conduct between both of them.

Thus, the silent examination which had been carrying on so far did not last any longer. The curled up girl somehow transformed once again into a full-formed young woman and disappeared into the interiors of the house along with the maidservant. Apurva curled his hardly grown moustache with a terribly grim expression on his face and got ready to step out of the room. After reaching the door he did not find his new burnished pair of shoes in the spot where he had left them, nor could he fathom out where they actually were, even after a great deal of thought.

The girl's family was extremely embarrassed and a volley of abuses and unkind words were showered on the unknown culprit in plenty. After a great deal of searching, Apurva had no other option but to put on the old, worn out and loose pair of slippers used by the master of the house along with his well-dressed countenance consisting of a coat, a pantaloon and turban. It was in this manner that Apurva stepped out extremely carefully on the muddy village path.

Whilst walking back Apurva heard once again the well-known high-pitched ripples of laughter directed at him when he passed the lonely wayside beside the lake. It appeared as if the witty goddess of the forest could not hold back her laughter looking at Apurva's incongruous pair of shoes.

Embarrassed to the hilt, Apurva stopped on his way and began looking here and there when suddenly a shamelessly guilty girl appeared from within the dense forests and kept his new pair of shoes before him before trying to flee from the spot. But Apurva quickly caught hold of her two arms and imprisoned the girl.

Mrinmayi struggled to escape his hands but did not succeed. From beyond the branches of the trees sun rays illuminated her curly haired, healthy, smiling impish face. Like an inquisitive traveller bends to look at the bottom of a sunlit, clear, playful water spring, so Apurva looked into Mrinmayi's uptilted face and liquid limpid eyes deeply and grimly, then very slowly loosened his grip on her and set her free as if keeping his mission incomplete in the process. Mrinmayi would never be surprised if Apurva would beat her in a rage but she failed to understand this beautiful, silent punishment amidst this lonely path.

The echoes of that playful laughter kept ringing all around the skies like the jingle of the dancing Mother Nature's anklets and a very thoughtful Apurva Krishna entered his home in slow footsteps.

III

Apurva, under some pretext or other, did not go to the interiors of the house to meet his mother the whole day.

There was an invitation outside so he attended to it. It is perhaps difficult to comprehend why an accomplished, serious and sensitive man like Apurva was so greatly anxious to prove his characteristic greatness to a simple, illiterate young girl and gain his lost glory once again. What was lost if a playful girl from a village did think he was like any other ordinary mortal? If the girl had made him a laughing stock for a moment and then simply forgot about his existence, showing an eagerness to play with a silly illiterate boy like Rakhal instead, how did it really matter to him? What was the necessity to prove to the girl that he was a book reviewer in a monthly journal called *Viswadeep* and his chest contained items like essence, shoes, camphor from Rubini, coloured paper meant for letter-writing and a voluminous notebook along with a book on 'How to learn playing a harmonium'—waiting like the expectant dawn eager to reveal itself from the womb of the dark night. But it was tough to explain these things to one's heart and Sir Apurva Krishna Roy, BA, was not at all prepared to admit defeat at the hands of a playful, simple, illiterate village girl.

When he entered the interiors of the house in the evening his mother asked "So Apu, how was the girl? Did you like her?"

Apurva answered a trifle unnerved, "I have seen some girls, Mother, and I have chosen one amongst them all." Mother was astonished and asked, "How come you have seen so many girls?" Ultimately, after a lot of hesitation, it was revealed that her son had chosen neighbouring Sarat's daughter Mrinmayi. That her highly educated son could have such taste was really quite incomprehensible!

Although Apurva was quite shy in the beginning, he got over it when his mother tried to vehemently oppose his decision. He stubbornly insisted that he would marry Mrinmayi, and no one else. Whenever he thought of the other lifeless dummy of a girl his mind would fill with utter resentment at the idea of marriage itself.

After two or three days of heartburn, emotional turmoil and remaining without food, it was Apurva who won the tussle eventually. The mother reconciled to the fact thinking that since Mrinmayi was too young and her mother was not capable of providing for her education, things would probably change once Mrinmayi got married and came into her very own domain. And, consequently, she also began to believe that Mrinmayi had a pretty face. At the next moment, however, the girl's shortened locks of hair came to her mind and filled it with despair. But she still lived on the hope that with time she would be able to rectify this defect by tying the girl's hair tightly and massaging it with lots of hair oil to make it grow faster.

The people of the neighbourhood named this choice of Apurva's as *Apurva Pachando*.* Many loved the crazy Mrinmayi but no one would ever dream of her as their daughter-in-law.

Mrinmayi's father, Ishan Mazumdar, was duly informed. He was engaged in loading and unloading of cargo and selling tickets as a clerk in a steamer company operating from a small tin-roofed hut in a tiny station.

He shed tears silently when he heard of the wedding proposal for Mrinmayi. We would not be able to measure how much of those tears were shed for sorrow and how much for happiness.

---
* *Apurva* means unheard of and *Pachando* choice in Bengali

Ishan applied for leave to attend his daughter's wedding from the officer in the head office. But his leave application was rejected as the reason was not considered significant enough. So, he wrote a letter home asking for a postponement of the wedding till the *Pooja* holidays when he would probably get a week's leave. But Apurva's mother said she could not wait any longer as there were some auspicious dates this month.*

The hurt Ishan, being rejected from every side, once again engaged himself in weighing cargo and selling tickets.

Thereafter, Mrinmayi's mother and all the elderly women of the village began to advise Mrinmayi on her future duties day and night. They prohibited her from childish playfulness, fast movements, loud laughter, talking to young boys and eating every now and then, and fully succeeded in making the impending marriage appear like a nightmare. The worried, panic-stricken Mrinmayi felt she had been sentenced to lifelong imprisonment and thereafter hanging till death.

She turned her neck stiffly, stepped back like a stubborn pony and said, "I will not marry."

IV

But still she had to marry. Then the training period began. Mrinmayi's entire world was imprisoned within the four walls of the interiors where Apurva's mother resided in just one night.

The mother-in-law began with her reformation process. She put on a hardened demeanour and told her, "See dear, you are no little girl, remember such

---

* In India weddings are held on certain auspicious dates of some months

behaviour will not be tolerated in this house." Mrinmayi did not take mother-in-law's words in the right spirit. She thought if she was not free to behave as she willed, she would have to go somewhere else. She was not found in the afternoon next day. Search for her began all over. It was the traitor Rakhal who ultimately revealed the secret place where she had hidden herself. She was crouching in the discarded broken chariot of *Radhakanto Thakur** in the shade of the banyan tree.

The readers can easily imagine how her mother-in-law, mother and well-wishers in the locality chided and admonished Mrinmayi.

It began to cloud densely that night and rain poured in big drops. Apurva Krishna went a little closer to Mrinmayi very softly and hesitatingly in the bed and murmured in her ears, "Mrinmayi, don't you love me?"

Mrinmayi spoke out forcefully, "No. I will never love you." She thrust all her anger and sense of punishment rolled as if into an assembled ball of thunder on poor Apurva's head.

Apurva, disappointed, said, "Why, what harm have I done?" Mrinmayi replied, "Why did you marry me?"

It was difficult to give a suitable answer for such an offence. But Apurva thought to himself, he would have to tame this impertinent girl somehow or the other.

The next day mother-in-law observed Mrinmayi's revolting mood and locked her in. She began to move here and there as impatiently as a newly caged bird flutters its wings. At last, seeing no way to escape, she bit the bedsheet in her fit of helpless anger and tore it to bits and pieces, and then stretched on the floor and began to call out to her father and weep.

---

* Lord Krishna known as the lover of Radha or *Radhakanto*

At that moment slowly someone came and sat beside her. Affectionately, he picked up her fallen hair and tried settling it above her cheeks. Mrinmayi vehemently shook her head, thereby moving away his hands. Apurva bent his face near her ears and murmured, "I have secretly opened the door. Come let us escape from the back door to the garden outside." Mrinmayi shook her head vehemently and said forcefully yet tearfully, "No". Apurva picked up her chin and tried to raise her face, "Just see who has come!" Rakhal was standing fixedly at the door staring at the fallen Mrinmayi. Mrinmayi did not look up and pushed off Apurva's hand. Apurva said, "Rakhal has come to play with you, won't you play with him?" She replied emotionally yet annoyingly, "No". Rakhal too felt that things were not really hunky-dory and somehow left the room in a huff, relieved to run from the scene. Apurva sat down quietly. Mrinmayi cried herself to sleep. Then Apurva went out on tiptoes chaining the room from outside.

The next day Mrinmayi received a letter from her father. He had expressed grief that he could not be present at his very dear Mrinmayi's wedding and had sent his heartfelt blessings for the newly-weds.

Mrinmayi went and told her mother-in-law, "I will go to my father." The mother-in-law began to admonish her for this sudden request of hers, "God knows where her father stays, and she says she will go to her father. Never heard of such a strange request." She went away without a reply, locked herself in her room and began to cry just as a pessimistic person prays to God pleadingly, "Baba, take me away. I won't live if I stay here longer."

Metamorphosis

In the late night hours when her husband slept Mrinmayi opened the door very slowly and went out of the house. Though it was sometimes getting cloudy there was enough moonlight to show the way. Mrinmayi knew nothing of the way which would lead to her father's place. But she had this strong belief that one could reach any address in this world by using the path tread by the postmen, also known as the 'runners'. Mrinmayi began walking the same path used by them. Her body grew weary after some walking and the night drew to an end. Inside the deep forest one or two birds were about to chirp hesitatingly not knowing the right time of the morning. At that very moment Mrinmayi reached the end of the road and found herself by the riverside in a huge market-place. She was thinking which way to go when she heard the familiar clanging sound (made by the bells the runners tie to their feet). Carrying the letter bag on his shoulders the runner came panting. Mrinmayi went near him and said in a painfully weary voice, "I want to go to my father in Kushiganj, why don't you take me along with you?" The man said, "I do not know where Kushiganj is?" Saying this he woke up the boatman in the postal boat tied to the anchor and started off in the boat. He had no time to question her or have pity on her.

Very soon the surrounding market-place woke up. Mrinmayi descended the embankment and called out to the boatman, "Boatman, will you take me to Kushiganj?" Before he could reply someone from the next boat cried out, "Oh! Is it our Minoo ma, how come you are here?" Mrinmayi spoke out intensely anxious, "Banamali, I will go to Kushiganj to see my father, take me in your boat." Banamali was a boatman from her village and he knew this indisciplined, wild-natured girl very well. So he asked, "Will you go to your father? That's nice. Come, I will take you there." Mrinmayi boarded the boat.

The boat began to sail. Suddenly clouds gathered and heavy rain lashed across. The river full to its brim in the *Bhadra** month began to sway the boat.

Mrinmayi's body grew weary with sleep; she spread her saree end on the floor of the boat and lay down. Very soon this terrible wild girl began to sleep peacefully like a happy, affectionately cared-for baby in the swaying boat.

When she woke up she found herself lying on a cot in her in-law's place. The maid began to scold her as soon as she woke up. Hearing the maid's voice her mother-in-law came in blurting strong words at her. Mrinmayi could only stare at her face with her widely opened eyes. But when consequently she made a dig at the defects in her father's training, Mrinmayi went running to the next room and bolted the door chain from inside.

Apurva gave up all his shame and told his mother, "Mother what is wrong if my wife is sent to her father's place for a day or two?"

His mother began to curse her fate and blamed Apurva that he had brought this irritating, headstrong girl home when there were so many better eligible girls in this country.

V

That day it was stormy and rainy outside, and a calamity of a similar kind was happening inside the room too.

---
* monsoon month of August–September in the Bengali calendar

The next night, deep into it, Apurva slowly woke up Mrinmayi and asked, "Mrinmayi, will you go to your father?"

Mrinmayi forcefully caught hold of Apurva's hand wideawake and said, "I'll go." Apurva asked in a soft tone, "Then come, let us both run away slowly. I have kept the boat ready."

Mrinmayi looked up to her husband's face gratefully. Then she got up quickly and dressed up to go out. Apurva left a letter for his mother to dispel her worries and then both of them started off.

That dark night in the deserted, quiet and desolate village path Mrinmayi, for the first time, caught hold of her husband's hand in complete faith wilfully. Her heartfelt joy and anxiety was communicated through that soft touch to the nerve cells of her husband.

The boat left that night itself. Although she was charged with a feeling of impatient joyousness, Mrinmayi fell asleep very soon. What fun the next day did bring! What freedom! So many villages and markets on both sides, farmlands, forests; so many boats going and coming on both sides! Mrinmayi kept on asking her husband every little insignificant thing several times. Who was travelling in which boat, from where had they come, what was the name of the place they were passing by—such questions the answers to which Apurva would not find in any of his college books and of which he did not have any experience. Readers would be ashamed to know that Apurva had answered all these questions one by one, and none of these answers had any semblance to truth. For instance, he had not hesitated to call a boat made out of a certain object as something else or Panchbere as *Rainagar**or the *munsif*

---
* names of villages

court as the office of a *zamindar** And the faithful girl's heart had not lost any of its joy even at his wrong answers.

The next evening the boat touched Kushiganj. A bare-chested Ishan Chandra was sitting on a stool and writing accounts keeping a huge leather-bound notebook on a small desk in a tin-roofed room with an oil lamp burning in a stained square-glassed lantern. At that moment the newly wed couple entered the room. Mrinmayi called out, 'Baba!' Such a touching voice had never resounded in that room ever before.

Ishan's eyes shed incessant tears. He did not know what to say or what to do. His daughter and son-in-law appeared to him as the princess and prince of an empire; he could not seem to figure out how a fitting throne could be constructed for them amongst all these jute bundles.

The next problem was food. A poor clerk like him who would cook rice and pulses together for his meal—how would he entertain on such a happy day? Mrinmayi said, "Baba, today we shall all cook together". Apurva expressed great enthusiasm at this proposal.

The room had a dearth of space, of helping hands and there was poverty all around. But joy and happiness began to flow out from that narrow source with such force that it looked like a fountain had been unleashed from a narrow mouth and had shot forth in all directions.

Three days passed this way. Steamers would come there regularly in the morning and evening and the place would echo with lot of people and a great deal of noise. But in the evening when the riverbed would become absolutely desolate, it meant total freedom to

---

* rich landlords ruling over other common villagers

do whatever one liked. And then the three of them would find a lot of ingredients, make a great deal of blunders and ultimately cook one item instead of another. And later it would be sitting for dinner with Mrinmayi serving them with a lot of care moving her bangled arms. The father-in-law and son-in-law would crack jokes at the imperfection of her wifely role and the girl would playfully express false indignation and objection to that.

At last Apurva said that it would not be wise to stay any longer. Mrinmayi sadly prayed for a few more days. But Ishan said, "No need."

On the day of departure Ishan pulled his daughter to his chest and put a hand on her head and said in a tear-laden voice, "My dear, stay put in your father-in-law's place just as the Goddess Lakshmi resides in all her glory and light. No one should point a finger at my Minoo."

Mrinmayi took farewell weeping all the time and went away with her husband. And Ishan went back to his old, now doubly joyless, narrow room weighing cargo day after day.

VI

When these two culprits returned home the mother kept a grim exterior and never said a word. She never accused any one of any kind of misbehaviour. Thus, there was no way to prove one's innocence. This silent complaint, this quiet rebellion seemed to weigh upon the entire family like an iron burden.

When it grew unbearable Apurva came and said, "Mother, the college is about to reopen, I must go and study law."

Mother said rather indifferently, "What should I do with your wife?"

Apurva said, "Let my wife stay with you." Mother said, "No, my dear, no need. You take her with you only." She was rather formal in her way of speaking to Apurva.

Apurva answered rather disappointed and hurt, "Fine".

Preparations were being made for leaving for Calcutta. The night before he was to leave Apurva found Mrinmayi on the bed, crying.

He was struck by this and asked sadly "Mrinmayi, don't you want to come with me to Calcutta?"

Mrinmayi answered, "No".

Apurva asked, "Don't you love me?" He did not get any reply now. Sometimes answering this question can be extremely easy but at times this question contained some such complicated consolation that one could not expect any reply from the girl.

Apurva questioned, "Do you feel sad to leave Rakhal and go?"

Mrinmayi answered easily, "Yes".

This graduated, accomplished young man suddenly felt a delicate needle-like prick of jealously for the little Rakhal. He then said, "I will not be able to come back home for a pretty long time." Mrinmayi had nothing to say about this very piece of information. Then Apurva further said, "Perhaps two years or more". Mrinmayi merely commented, "When you come back bring a three-cornered knife for Rakhal."

Apurva rose a little from his bed and said, "So you will stay put here?" Mrinmayi replied, "Yes, I want to go and stay with my mother."

Apurva sighed and said, "Fine. I will never come back till you write to me asking me to come. Does that please you?"

Mrinmayi did not consider this question worth answering and perhaps fell asleep. But Apurva could not sleep, he set up the pillow and kept on sitting upright. Late at right the moon rose and the moonlight fell on the bed. Apurva looked at Mrinmayi in that light. She appeared as a sleeping princess touched by a silver magic wand—as if a golden magic wand would wake up this unconscious apparition and then he could exchange *garlands**** with her. The silver wand signified laughter, and the golden tears.

Apurva woke up Mrinmayi in the early morning and said, "Mrinmayi it is time for me to go. Come let me take you to your mother's house."

When Mrinmayi got up from the bed Apurva caught hold of both her hands and said, "Now I have a request. I have helped you many times in many ways, today will you give me a reward for that?"

Mrinmayi asked, bewildered, "What?"

Apurva said, "Willingly and lovingly, do plant a kiss on my lips."

Mrinmayi laughed aloud at hearing Apurva's strange plea but seeing the grim expression on his face. she controlled herself and moved nearer to kiss him but as she grew closer she could not hold herself and chuckled aloud. In this way she tried twice but ultimately gave up and began to laugh covering her face with the end of her *saree*†. Apurva disciplined her playfully by slowly pulling her earlobes.

---

* malabadal or exchanging of flower garlands is a form of wedding rite
† a nine-yard long material draped around the body of an Indian woman

Apurva had taken a solemn vow. He thought it was ignominy to ask for love through sheer brutal force. He wanted love to be presented to him on a platter as if served to God—he did not wish to take it himself.

Mrinmayi did not laugh any more. Travelling through the desolate village path in the faint day, light, he left her in her mother's place. Apurva returned home and told his mother, "I thought over it and came to the conclusion that if I took my wife with me to Calcutta my studies would be hampered. Moreover, she does not have any companion there. Since you do not want to keep her here I left her at her mother's place."

Mother and son grew apart because of a deep misunderstanding.

VII

After coming to her mother's house Mrinmayi discovered that she was not able to concentrate on anything. It seemed as if that house had changed completely. Time never seemed to pass. She did not know what to do, where to go or whom to meet.

Suddenly Mrinmayi felt that there was no one in the house and in the entire village—as if the sun had eclipsed in mid-afternoon. She just could not comprehend why the past night she had not felt this sudden desire to go to Calcutta as she was feeling right now. She did not know the day before that the world where she had belonged and which she was sorely missing had undergone a total transformation within this short time. Today she threw away her past life as easily as a dry leaf falls off from the branches of a tree.

One hears of stories where the expert blacksmith builds such a sharp sword that when it cuts a man into two, the man does not know it until the body is shaken and the two half pieces fall apart. The Almighty's sword was just as sharp and fine. Mrinmayi had not known when He had dealt the blow segregating her childhood and her youth. Today with a sudden jolt her childhood fell apart from her youth and Mrinmayi kept on viewing it with utter surprise and an unknown pain in her heart.

She could not think of her old bedroom in her mother's house as her own any more, the one who had been living there suddenly seemed to have disappeared. Now all her memories seemed to resolve musically around that other house, that specific room and the other bed.

No one else sees Mrinmayi anywhere outside. No one ever hears her resounding laughter. Rakhal too stays away from her now. He does not dare to play with her.

Mrinmayi asked her mother, "Ma, leave me at my in-laws."

On the other hand, Apurva's mother's heart broke into two whenever she remembered her departing son's sad face. That her son had been cross with her and had left his wife in her mother's place hurt her no end.

Almost at that time Mrinmayi came in with a pale face and a veil over her head and fell at her feet to show obeisance. The mother-in-law immediately took her in her arms with tears in her eyes. Both united in a single moment. The mother-in-law was surprised to see the change in Mrinmayi's face. She had transformed. Such change was not possible for all. One needed great strength of mind for such great change within oneself.

The mother-in-law had decided that she would rectify Mrinmayi's flaws one by one, but another invisible power had already adopted some unknown and faster method to create a new birth for Mrinmayi. Such was the transformation!

Now it was far easier for Mrinmayi to understand her mother-in-law, and for the latter to really understand her. It was almost as if a conciliation had occurred between the huge tree and its branches—such was the united manner in which the household now began to run onwards.

This solemn yet sweet all-pervading feminity which filled up every corner of Mrinmayi's body and soul seemed to pain her a lot. Like the newly evolved, dark, wet clouds at the onset of monsoons her heart suddenly awoke to a sorrowful feeling, misunderstanding. This feeling cast a deeper shadow over her shady long eyelashes. She began to whisper to herself,"It is true that I did not know myself. But why didn't you try to understand me? Why didn't you punish me? Why didn't you mould me the way you wanted? When I, being a stupid woman refused to go along with you to Calcutta, why did you listen to me, why did you obey my request, why did you bear with my disobedience?"

And later, she remembered how Apurva had looked only once at her after arresting her in his arms in that lonely path in the shores of the lake that morning. She remembered that path, shade of those trees, that morning and that deep glance laden with feelings and suddenly realised the significance of it all. And then the incomplete goodbye kiss which had proceeded towards Apurva's lips but was taken back now seemed to continuously go back to the past days as thirsty as a bird heading for the oasis in a desert. Nothing seemed to quench that thirst. Now and then she kept thinking what she could have done that time, what answer she should have given to that question, if only such a thing would have happened?

Apurva had suffered from the grievance that Mrinmayi did not know him fully. Today Mrinmayi too thinks how her husband had failed to understand her, how he must have felt. She was aggrieved at the thought that Apurva had found Mrinmayi as only an impatient, fun-loving, unthinking little girl. He never knew her as a full-blooded woman who could fulfill the thirst for love with the elixir of life stored within herself. This seemed to shake her entire being with shame and regret. She paid back those unexpressed debts of kisses and lovemaking on Apurva's pillow instead of him. Some days passed by in this way.

Apurva had said unless she writes he would not return. Remembering that, Mrinmayi shut the door one day and began writing a letter. She took out the coloured paper bordered with gold given by Apurva and began thinking. Very carefully in crooked lines and ink on her fingers, writing some letters small and some big and without any form of address, she wrote, "Why don't you write to me. How are you and now you come home." She could not think what more to write. She had written all that she had wanted to say, but in human society affairs of the heart need to be expressed with more clarity. Mrinmayi too understood this, and thus after a lot of thinking she added a few more words, "Now you write to me. And also write how you are, and come home. Mother is fine, Bishu, Puty is fine. Yesterday our black cow has delivered a calf." Then she stopped writing. Later she wrapped the letter in an envelope and then wrote his name—each letter containing drops of her love—Shree Babu Apurva Krishna Roy. She had sent her love in it but the spelling was incorrect, lines were not straight and the letters not symmetrical.

Mrinmayi did not know that one had to write anything besides the name on the envelope. Lest her mother-in-law or anyone else sees it she quickly sent the letter with her faithful servant to post.

Needless to say there was no reaction to this letter for Apurva did not come home.

VIII

Mother noticed that Apurva did not come home even for the holidays. She thought he was still cross with her.

Even Mrinmayi realised that Apurva was quite annoyed with her and she died with shame at the thought of the letter she had written. How insignificant that letter was; so many things had not been written and so many feelings had remained unexpressed! She suffered, struck by arrows from within thinking how after reading that letter Apurva must be thinking that she was an immature, stupid girl and an object worth ignoring. She kept on asking the maid, "Have you posted that letter?" The maid answered her several times in the imperative, "Yes, Yes. I have myself put it into the letter box. *'Babu'** must have got it long back."

At last Apurva's mother called, Mrinmayi one day and said, "Bouma, Apu has not come home for quite some time. So I am thinking of going and meeting him in Calcutta. Will you come with me?" Mrinmayi nodded her head in the affirmative—went inside her room, bolted the door, fell on the bed clutching the pillow to

---
* equivalent of Sir—a respectful address in Bengali

her chest and laughed and rolled around in a fit of emotional outburst. Then later she slowly turned serious and sat sadly for some time full of apprehensions and then began to cry.

These two repentant ladies set off for Calcutta to beg forgiveness without informing Apurva. Apurva's mother put up with her son-in-law in Calcutta.

That evening after waiting for Mrinmayi's letter in vain, Apurva had broken his vow and started writing a letter to Mrinmayi. No words seemed to please him. He was searching for a form of address which would express love and yet reveal the inner feeling inside him. He was getting distressed with his mother tongue as he was failing to find the appropriate word for his specific emotion. Suddenly he received a letter from his brother-in-law stating that Mother had come and he must visit her very soon and have dinner with them. Everything was fine. In spite of the ending words, Apurva panicked with anxiety and immediately landed up at his sister's residence.

He visited his mother and asked her, "Ma, hope everything is fine?" Ma answered, "All fine. You did not come home for the holidays so I have come to take you home."

Apurva muttered, "What was the need to come all the way just for this? You know what studying for law exams means... ."

While eating his sister asked him "Dada, why didn't you bring your wife with you?"

The brother grimly replied, "Studying for law... ." The brother-in-law remarked, "All those are false excuses. He fears to bring his wife before us." The sister said, "You are really a horrifying man. A small girl would definitely coil at the sight of you."

The evening carried on in light spirit of fun and laughter, but Apurva remained sad and grim. He was not interested in any kind of conversation. He was thinking Mrinmayi could have easily accompanied his mother when she had taken the trouble to come to Calcutta. Perhaps his mother had tried to bring her but she did not agree. He could not ask his mother on this topic out of embarrassment—the entire world seemed to be full of contradictions to him.

After dinner, extreme winds gave way to heavy outpour outside. His sister said, "Dada, stay here with us tonight."

Dada said, "No, I must go home. I have some work left."

The brother-in-law said, "What work do you do in such late hours? You do not have to explain to anyone at home if you stay here overnight. So why do you worry?"

After a lot of cajoling Apurva agreed to stay that night much against his wishes.

The sister said, "Dada, you look so tired, do not delay—just go to bed." Even Apurva wished so. He would be relieved to be alone in the darkness of his bedroom, he was in no mood to converse with anyone.

He came to the door of the bedroom and found it dark. The sister said, "The light seemed to have blown off. Should I bring you a lamp?"

Apurva said, "Not required. I do not light a lamp while retiring to bed."

After the sister left Apurva went carefully towards the bed.

As he was about to climb the bed a pair of soft arms caught him in a tight embrace with the sound of jangling bangles and two lips like rose petals came over his lips forcefully and overwhelmed him with a tearful and highly emotional heavenly kiss. The whole action was so swift that he did not even get an opportunity to express surprise. Though shocked at first, Apurva soon realised that an incomplete action which had been interrupted by peals of laughter had now been completed this time washed in tears.

☆☆☆☆☆

Six

Punishment
Shasti

I

When the two brothers Dukhiram Rui and Chidam Rui started out in the morning—axes in their hands all set for their daily labour; their wives were screaming and squabbling with each other. But the people of the locality had become quite accustomed to these noisy bickerings—now an everyday phenomenon akin to the other variety of sounds created by Mother Nature. Now whenever a sharp noise arose anywhere people would say, "There again it begins"—meaning that what had been expected had happened and that there had been no change in the normal behavioural pattern. Just as no one questions the reason behind the sun rising in the east in the morning so also no one expressed curiosity at knowing the reasons behind this huge commotion taking place between these two sisters-in-law of this Kuri household.

This quarrelling and squabbling affected the two husbands much more than the neighbours no doubt; but they did not consider it disadvantageous at all. It seemed as if these two brothers were travelling in a single carriage all through this long, worldly trip and had accepted the continuous screeching and jarring noise of the two wheels devoid of any spring on either side as the preordained characteristic of the chariot of life moving ahead on its destined journey.

On the other hand, whenever there would be utter silence all around and every thing would be still and calm an ominous fear of some unexpected, unnatural event about to occur would fill their hearts. No one could predict what would happen or when on such a day.

Our story begins when, one early evening the two brothers returned home weary after heavy labour and found the entire household immersed in a weird, ominous silence.

It was quite humid outside as well. It had rained heavily at about two in the afternoon. The sky was still enveloped with clouds. There was no trace of a breeze anywhere. Due to monsoon thick vegetation and shrubs had grown considerably surrounding the house from all sides. A dense smell arising out of the dampness of the foliage and the flooded jute fields nearby had engulfed the surroundings like an invincible stone wall. The frogs were croaking from the pond at the backyard of the cowshed and the calm evening sky was kept awake by the steady chiring of crickets.

A little further, the river Padma had assumed a terribly still and ominously-darkened countenance under the clouded shadowy sky of this rainy afternoon. A large portion of the grain fields had been washed away thus coming closer to human habitation. And the few mango and jackfruit trees which had left their roots behind in that corner of disintegration appeared like the spread out fingers of some helpless fist trying to cling on to some kind of a last resort but only in vain.

That very day Dukhiram and Chidam had gone to the office of the local zamindar for work. The paddy grown in damp land was just ready for harvesting in the marshy fields on other side. Most of the poor in this countryside had been appointed by the landlord to work in their own paddy fields or in jute plantations in order to reap the crop before the land was washed away by the rains. But only these two brothers were forcefully summoned by the guards of the zamindar and taken to his office. They had had to work the whole day trying to repair the leaking roof of the office room and constructing a few mat doors. They had not been able to return home and had eaten just a little in their place of work. Moreover, they had had to get wet in the drizzle and had not received due wages for their labour. Instead, they had been more than compensated for their lawful dues by quite a few harsh and unjust words.

After wading through the muddy roads flooded with water the two brothers returned home in the evening to find the younger sister-in-law Chandara lying quietly on the floor spreading out the end of her saree. Like the cloudy day today, she too had shed a volley of tears the entire afternoon and had given a break to the incessant crying towards the evening and was right now in a calm and still state. The elder sister-in-law Radha had assumed a heavy countenance and was sitting in the verandah. Her young son aged a year and a half was crying. When the two brothers entered they saw the naked child lying headlong in a corner of the courtyard fast asleep.

The hungry Dukhiram did not pause for a while and immediately ordered, "Give me my meal of rice"; The wife burst into flames of anger almost like a gunny bag which had caught fire and screamed out loudly in her sharp voice almost at once; "Where is the 'rice' that I should serve? Had you given me rice before you left? Do I earn for the family from now onwards?"

After going through an entire day of hard work and utter disgrace, stepping into this miserably-dark home troubled by a belly burning with hunger, Dukhiram could not bear to hear his wife's harsh voice specially the ugly sarcasm hidden in her last words any longer. He roared aloud like an angry tiger "What did you say?" As he uttered these words he picked up a chopper and without giving a thought struck his wife on her head within fraction of a second. Radha fell near the lap of her younger sister-in-law and breathed her last almost instantaneously.

Soaked in blood Chandara cried out aloud, "Oh my—what has happened!" Chidam covered her mouth. Dukhiram let go of the chopper and thumped on the floor without a word—a hand over his mouth. The child woke up and began crying aloud in fear.

It was serenely quiet outside at that hour. The cowboy was returning to his village with the cattle. The five or seven people who had crossed the river to cut the harvest on the other side had returned one by one in small boats and were now heading for home with a few bales of paddy on their heads as reward for their whole day's toil.

Ramlochan *Khuro** of the Chakraborty household had posted letters in the village post office and was peacefully smoking tobacco after returning home. He suddenly remembered that his subtenant, Dukhi, owed him a fair amount of tax and had promised to pay a part of it tonight. Thinking that the two brothers would have returned home by now he draped the shawl upon his shoulder; took out the umbrella and started out.

He could see that the evening lamp had not been lit as yet. A fewrather, obscure, human figures could be seen sitting in the darkness of the evening.

---

* father's brother or 'uncle' in Bengal

Every now and then a stifled moaning sound could be heard from the corner—whenever the small child cried, 'Ma Ma!' Chidam was hurriedly shutting him up.

Ramlochan, rather taken aback, called out, "Dukhi are you at home?"

Dukhi was sitting still like a stone statue all along. Hearing his name being called aloud he wept out like a small kid.

Chidam quickly came down to the courtyard nearer to Chakraborty. Chakraborty questioned, "Have the bitches quarrelled again? I heard them screaming the whole day!"

Till now Chidam had not been able to figure out what to do. A bevy of weird ideas had been crossing his head. For the moment he had decided that he would remove the dead body somewhere else as the night deepened. He had never dreamt that Chakraborty would suddenly arrive. Hence he could not think what to answer and said without thinking, "Yes, yes, today they have squabbled quite a lot".

Chakraborty attempted to move towards them saying, "But why is Dukhi crying for that?"

Chidam guessed that they would now be caught. So he blurted out, "*Chotobou** has struck *Borobou* on her head with an axe as retaliation."

One never thinks of any other danger besides the immediate one. At that moment Chidam was planning how he would get rid of the terrible truth. That the falsehood could be even worse did not enter his head. He had blurted out the only answer which had occurred to him at that moment when Ramlochan had questioned him.

---

* young, married women of the household are addressed by elders as such

Ramlochan shuddered and exclaimed, "What! What are you saying! Has she died?"

Chidam mumbled, "Yes she's dead"—and then caught hold of Chakraborty's feet tightly.

Chakraborty did not know what to do. He thought, "Oh my good Lord, what trouble have I landed into this evening! Now my life will be at stake what with appearing at the witness-box in court" and so on... Chidam did not let go of his feet. He said, "Dada Thakore, how will I save my wife now?"

Ramlochan was the prime advisor of the village in matters of law and court cases. He thought for a while and said, "See, there is a way. You run to the police station now itself and say that your elder brother Dukhi had asked for rice and had struck his wife fatally on finding that the rice had not been prepared. I can say for sure that the girl will be saved if you say this."

Chidam's throat parched. He said "Thakore, I will get another wife if this one goes. But if my brother is hanged, I will never get another." He had not thought of these excuses when he had put the blame on his wife. Now his heart was secretly trying to defend his own actions through reason and logic.

Even Chakraborty thought his arguments were logical. So he said, "Then just relate what exactly had happened. It is quite impossible to hide all the possible angles of this case".

Saying this, Ramlochan took leave immediately. Very soon, word spread throughout the entire village that Chandara of the Kuri household had struck her elder sister-in-law with an axe in a fit of rage.

Just as water gushes out of a damaged dam, so did the police force rush into the village—the culprit and the innocent both began to grow worried at this phenomenon.

II

Chidam thought he would now have to tread the path which he himself had created. He could not figure out what he should say or do now. He had himself related a fabricated story to Chakraborty and by now the entire village had come to know of it. Now if he said something different who knows what could happen—he himself did not know. So he thought he must keep that version intact, perhaps adding a few more stories to it in order to save his wife.

Chidam requested his wife Chandara to shoulder the burden of the crime.

The woman was absolutely dumbstruck. Chidam tried to assure her saying, "Do whatever I am saying, do not fear, we will save you"—Although he promised her so his throat was parched and his face grew pale.

Chandara's age would not exceed seventeen or eighteen. Her face was rounded and plump and her figure was short yet healthy and terse. There was a certain charm in her physique which made all her movements very flexible and graceful. Almost like a newly constructed boat—quite small and well-built—one which could move about effortlessly and one in which there were no joints which had become loose. She possessed a good deal of humour and curiosity about almost any subject on this earth. She loved to chat with neighbours; and while going and coming to the river 'ghat' with a water jug balanced on her waist, she would see all that was interesting on the way with her bright, restless dark black eyes through a small gap created in her veil by her own two fingers.

Borobou was just the opposite—extremely disorganised, indisciplined and lethargic. She could not handle the veil on her head, neither could she look after the boy on her lap nor worry about household duties. She did not have any work to do but still she could never ever relax. The younger sister-in-law had stopped talking much, only rebuking her in soft yet biting words but the elder sister-in-law in answer would make a huge scene by quarrelling, crying and screaming in anger thereby disturbing the entire locality.

There was a curious unity in the nature of these two couples. Dukhiram was of a heavier build—his bone structure was quite broad, the nose blunt and his two eyes seemed to say that they did not quite fathom what this visible world was all about but could not question it either. Such a timid yet forceful, strong yet helpless man is seldom found.

And Chidam seemed to have been sculpted by someone with immense care out of shining black stone. There was no trace of extravagance anywhere and no blemish was to be found anywhere in his muscular body. Every part of his physique had attained perfection as if they matched his inert strength and efficiency. Whether it was leaping down from the higher banks of a river, or pushing the pulleys of a boat or climbing a bamboo plant to carefully select bamboo shoots or any other job, he accomplished them all with a kind of controlled perfection and a carefree style. He had taken great care to brush his deep black, long oily hair away from his forehead to frame around his shoulders. He was definitely conscious about his dress and appearance.

Though he was not indifferent towards the beauty of the other women of the village and was also quite eager to make himself presentable to them, Chidam loved his young wife in a special way. Both of them quarrelled and made up too—none could outdo the other. And, there was one more reason for the strong bond between the two. Chidam would think one could not trust a frisky, restless woman like Chandara enough, and Chandara on the other hand would think that her husband was quite a philanderer and if she did not keep him in reins there was no knowing when he would slip away.

Some time before this particular incident the husband and wife had been undergoing a turmoil amongst themselves. Chandara had seen that her husband would sometimes go away on the pretext of work and even spend one or two days somewhere yet come back without any income. Seeing such misdemeanour, she too began to exhibit some misconduct. She began to go to the river for bath every now and then, roam all around the neighbourhood and come back all praise for the second son of Shri Kashi Mazumdar.

Someone seemed to have mingled poison to Chidam's days and nights. He was not able to rest in peace either at work or anywhere else. Once he had come back and chided his elder sister-in-law. She had waved her hand and cried out addressing the absent dead father of hers saying, "That woman runs ahead of the thunderstorm—how do I control her! I know one day she will create serious trouble."

Chandara had suddenly arrived from the next room and said in a slow menacing tone, "Why Didi, why do you fear such?" At this, once again the two of them had begun their fierce quarrel.

Chidam rolled his eyes and rebuked her, "If ever I hear that you have been alone to the river side, I will break your bones." Chandara replied, "Oh I will be relieved!" And, immediately she prepared to go out once again.

Chidam leaped up, pulled her hair, dragged her in and bolted the door from outside.

When he returned home from work in the evening he found the room open and no one inside. Chandara had, in the meantime, crossed three villages and reached her maternal uncle's house.

Chidam ultimately brought her back home after a fair deal of cajoling. This time he admitted defeat. He realised that just as it was difficult to hold a handful of sand in a tight grip, so also it was impossible to keep this chink of a girl tightly within his control—she seemed to trickle out through his fingers.

He did not dominate her any more but spent days in anxiety. His insecure, anxious love for his flirty young wife seemed to hurt him terribly like an old wound. So much so, that sometimes he felt that if she died at least he would be able to relax and attain eternal peace. A human being could be more envious of another much more than he would be of say, Yama, the Lord of Death.

At that moment this grievous incident occurred.

When her husband requested her to shoulder the charge of this murder, Chandara was stunned. Her two black eyes seemed to burn her husband silently like two burning pieces of black charcoal. Her entire being seemed to shrink trying to escape the clutches of this demon like husband of hers. Her spirit rebelled against him.

Chidam assured her, "You need not fear." Saying this he directed her on what she would have to tell the police and the magistrate several times. Chandara never quite heard his long story but sat still like a wooden statue.

Dukhiram depended on Chidam for everything. When Chidam asked Chandara to take the blame, Dukhi said, "Then what will happen to *Bouma*?" Chidam said, "I will release her somehow." The burly and strong Dukhiram was quite reassured.

III

Chidam had instructed his wife that she should say her elder sister-in-law had advanced towards her with a cutter to kill her and she had tried to protect herself with an axe but somehow it had hurt the former instead. All this was entirely Ramlochan's story. He had instructed Chidam in detail about what kind of verbal techniques and evidence would be required to prove this point.

The police arrived to investigate. The villagers were by now dead sure that it was Chandara who had murdered her elder sister-in-law. When the police questioned Chandara, she admitted, "Yes, I have killed her".

"What made you kill her?"

"I did not see eye to eye with her".

"Did you quarrel?"

"No."

"Did she try to hurt you?"

"No."

"Did she torture you?"

"No."

Her reply surprised all those who were present.

Chidam grew agitated. He said, "She is not saying the truth. Borobou first...."

The inspector stopped him with a dire threat. At last after legally cross-examining her several times he got the same reply, Chandara refused to admit that there had been any attack from her elder sister-in-law at any time.

Such a stubborn girl is rarely seen. She seemed to be bent upon welcoming the gallows—no one would be able to pull her back. Was this extreme sensitivity? Chandara seemed to be whispering to her husband in her heart, "I will leave you and welcome the hanging platform in my full-bloomed youth—that will be my eternal bond with life."

The imprisoned Chandara, an innocent, small, impishly naughty, young village woman carried a deeply imprinted mark of defame and walked through the well-known village path—through the area where the religious chariot stands and through the local market, crossing the river banks, passing the Mazumdar's house, the post office and the school building—the object of everyone's curiosity leaving her home for ever and ever. A bevy of boys followed her and the women and their friends peeping through their veils, some standing at their doorways and some standing behind the trees kept observing the arrested Chandara being led along by the police and shrinking within themselves in shame, disgust and fear.

Chandara admitted her crime even in front of the deputy magistrate. There was no revelation even now that Borobou had tortured her in some way just before the murder.

But, the same day Chidam came to the witness-box and cried out with folded hands, "Please sir, my wife has not done anything wrong." The judge stopped his emotional outburst with a snub and kept asking him several questions. Slowly, Chidam revealed the true facts.

The judge did not believe his words. The reason was, the main, reliable, gentlemanly witness Ramlochan had said, "I was present at the spot of action soon after the incident. The witness Chidam had admitted the entire episode and had requested me fervently to suggest some way of saving his wife from acquittal. But I had not committed anything. The witness again asked me, 'If I say in court that my elder brother had asked for his meal and when refused he had struck his wife in a fit of rage, will she then be freed?' I warned him, 'Beware, you rogue, do not utter a syllable of a lie in court—there is no greater sin than that.' etc."

At first, Ramlochan had made up quite a few stories to protect Chandara, but when Chandara herself stuck to the lie he thought to himself, 'O my God why should I go to jail for standing false witness now. It will be better to say what I already know'. And so Chidam dittoed only what Ramlochan had related. In fact, he did not hesitate to add more spice to the version.

The deputy magistrate transferred the case to the sessions court.

Meanwhile farming, marketing, tears and laughter—all the worldly activities went on as usual. And the incessant monsoon rains of the Sravana month showered on the green, fresh paddy fields as it always did through the years.

The police appeared in court along with the convict and the witness at the appointed hour. Innumerable people were in the munsiff court waiting for their own cases to mature. A lawyer had arrived from Calcutta to settle the case of distributing rights for a small pond behind a kitchen and thirty-nine witnesses were present on behalf of the plaintiff. So many kinds of people had come anxious to settle their own trivial scores to the minutest details. They perhaps thought that there was nothing more serious in the big big world. Chidam was looking at this terribly busy every day life cycle from the window—everything seemed to be like a dream. A cuckoo was calling out from the huge banyan tree in the corner of the compound—they did not have to worry about court or law. Chandara told the judge, "Oh please Sir, how many times do I have to utter the same story!"

The judge explained, "Do you know the punishment for the crime you have admitted to have done?"

Chandara said, "No".

The judge then said, "The punishment is hanging to death."

Chandara cried out, "Oh Sir, I fall on your feet, please do so. Do whatever you will, I can bear no more!"

When Chidam was brought to court, Chandara turned away. The judge told her, "Look at the witness and say who he is."

Chandara covered her face with both hands and said, "He is my husband".

She was asked—"Doesn't he love you?" The reply was—"Oh! Very much!". When the question was—"Don't you love him?" The answer was, "Very much".

When Chidam was asked, he said, "I have murdered her." When asked why he said, "I wanted rice but Borobou did not give me."

Dukhiram had come to be a witness. Suddenly he fell unconscious. After gaining consciousness he replied, "Sir, I have committed the murder." When asked why he too replied, "I wanted my meal of rice but she refused."

After going through several rounds of cross-questioning and listening to other witnesses, the judge could clearly understand that the two brothers were admitting to the crime just to save the woman of the household from the gallows. Chandara had been saying the same thing right from the police court to the session court, there had been no change in her version. Two lawyers had wilfully tried their utmost to save Chandara from the death sentence but had to give it up in the face of her determination.

When a darkish, short, childish girl with her rounded plump face had entered her in-laws' home leaving her coveted dolls at her father's home who ever would have imagined on that auspicious, ceremonial night that such a dreadful fate awaited her? Her father had died with the consolation that he had settled his daughter well.

Just before she was taken to the gallows the kind-hearted civil sergeant asked Chandara, "Do you wish to see anyone?"

Chandara said, "I want to see my mother just once."

The doctor said, "Your husband wants to see you, shall I call him?"

Chandara only replied, "What a shame!"

July-August, 1300

★★★★★

Seven

Penance
Prayaschitta

I

There is a certain place without any address hanging somewhere precariously between heaven and earth where the flowers of imagination abound in plenty. This imaginary continent surrounded by a fortress of airy nothings could be called "something which could have happened". Some have attained immortality through their noble actions and gained recognition. Some are not blessed with extraordinary powers and are successful only as ordinary men and it is only in ordinary everyday duties that they gain recognition. But the ones who have been caught in the midway between both by a queer play of fate are those who have no other alternative. They 'could have' become something great, but because of this very reason it was perhaps impossible for them to *'be something'*.

Our young friend Anathbandhu belonged to that unfortunate middle category. Everyone felt he would have succeeded in any field had he only wished to. But, he did not ever wish to do anything of that sort and thus he could not succeed in anything either. Hence faith on his undiscovered greatness remained forever intact. Everyone predicted that he would stand first in his exams; but he did not appear for any. Everyone believed that he would secure the highest position in any department once he joined a job; but unfortunately he did not accept a job. He ignored the common people since they were so very insignificant. Neither did he show the least respect towards the extraordinary ones, for he felt he could have been further extraordinary had he only wanted to be so.

All his fame and prosperity, happiness, wealth and good luck seemed to have been implied in the impossible reserve of 'something which could have happened'.

But the great Lord had bestowed two blessings on him for certain. They were a wealthy father-in-law and a gentle wife. The wife was named Vindyavasini.

Though Anathbandhu did not like his wife's name and he did not consider her suitably matched with himself either in beauty or in accomplishments, Vindyavasini was full of pride at her good fortune of having acquired a husband like him. That her husband was greater than all the husbands of all the wives in every possible way was something about which she had no doubt—neither did her husband himself. Even general opinion endorsed this view.

Vindyavasini would forever be apprehensive lest her pride in her husband ever gets even a little maimed. If she could install him in the highest peak of the lofty and indestructible mountains of devotion within her heart keeping him away from the evil eye of the ignorant wider world; perhaps she would be able to devote herself to the place of her husband in utmost peace. But in this inert lifeless world, it is perhaps impossible to place the object of worship on a pedestal. Moreover, there was no dearth of people who did not think of Anathbandhu as the ultimate model of a perfect youth. Vindyavasini herself had had to face a lot of anxieties because of this.

When Anathbandhu went to college he would live in his in-laws' house. When the date of examination arrived, he did not appear for them, and the next year he left college.

This incident embarrassed Vindyavasini no end. She softly told Anathbandhu that night, "You should've appeared for the exams."

Anathbandhu pooh-poohed her words and smilingly said, "Does one attain salvation just by appearing for exams? Even our Kedar has passed them!"

Vindyavasini was consoled. What would 'her' Anathbandhu achieve by sitting for an exam which a whole lot of other foolish, ignorant people had already cleared!

The neighbouring Kamala had gleefully arrived to give her childhood mate Bindi the good news that her brother Ramesh had passed the exams this time and received scholarship. But this made Vindyavasini unnecessarily suspicious that Kamala's joy was not totally unaffected and that there was a certain amount of sarcasm implied therein which was directed at her husband. Thus she did not express delight at her friend's joyous piece of news. On the other hand, she was quite offensive declaring in a quarrelsome tone that passing the L.A. exams was no great achievement at all. And also that there was no examination a stage lower than the BA in colleges abroad. Needless to say that Vindya had collected all this logical information from her husband.

Kamala was quite astonished and hurt to receive such a blow from her greatest friend when she had actually come to deliver some good news. But, she too was of the feminine species and so did not take long to comprehend what was going on in Vindyavasini's mind. She too was angered at the insult directed at her brother and hence spoke with words dripping with venom saying, "My dear, we people never went abroad nor married a foreigner; how would we know so much? I am only an illiterate woman—I only know that a Bengali boy has to appear for L.A. in college. Even that, my dear, is not everyone's cup of tea." Kamala told her friend these words very innocently and sweetly and later went away. Vindhya did not want to argue and thus bore her words quietly. Then she entered the room and wept in silence.

Another incident happened shortly thereafter. A distant, rich relation of theirs had come to Calcutta for some time and taken shelter in Vindyavasini's father's place. This arrival gave cause for a special ceremonious atmosphere in her father Rajkumar Babu's house. The son-in-law of the house was asked to vacate the huge drawing room which he usually occupied and requested to stay in her maternal uncle's room for a few days just to entertain these newly arrived guests.

Anathbandhu was greatly disturbed at this fact. At first he sharply criticised her father and made Vindyavasini cry thereby taking revenge on his father-in-law. Later he tried to show his temper by refusing to eat and several such tantrums. Vindyavasini was extremely embarrassed at this. With her natural sense of self-dignity she could sense that such a public display of emotions in such a situation could be the ultimate blow to self-respect. She coaxed and cajoled her husband to somehow keep him under control.

Vindya was not unreasonable and so she did not blame her parents. She knew that this kind of incident was quite natural and commonplace. But she even felt that her husband was being deprived of due care and affection which was expected from one's in-laws as he was staying with them all the time.

From that day onwards she began to tell her husband, "Please take me to your place, I do not wish to stay here anymore."

Anathbandhu was proud enough but had no self-respect. He had absolutely no desire to go back to the poverty of his own home. But his wife expressed her determination saying, "If you do not go, I will go myself."

Anathbandhu, inwardly annoyed, made arrangements to take his wife to his clay-built hay stacked hut in a far-off, small village somewhere in the outskirts of Calcutta. While leaving, Rajkumar Babu and his wife requested their daughter to stay a few days more. But their daughter sat quietly with her head bent and grimface silently letting them know that no, she would not do that.

Seeing her sudden determined decision her parents suspected that perhaps unwantingly she had been hurt by someone. With a heavy heart Rajkumar Babu asked her, "My dear, have we unknowingly hurt you in any way?"

Vindyavasini glanced at her father with sad eyes and said, "Not for a moment. I have spent my days in utmost luxury and comfort." Saying this she began to cry. But her decision was irrevocable.

The parents sighed and thought no matter how much of love and affection one showered on one's daughter, ultimately she turns into a stranger once she is married off.

At last, with tearful eyes Vindyavasini did goodbye to her father's home leaving her familiar affectionate surroundings, friends and companions and boarded the *'palki'**.

II

There is an insurmountable difference between an affluent household of the city of Calcutta and an ordinary household in a small village. But Vindhavasini never exhibited any signs of discomfort either in her behaviour or in her actions. She cheerfully began to assist her mother-in-law in the housework. Knowing that the family was not well-off her father had sent a maid along with his daughter on his own expenses. Vindyavasini sent her away as soon as she reached her in-law's home. She could not bear to think how this maid from an affluent family would inwardly scoff at the poverty of her in-laws every moment of the day.

The mother-in-law would affectionately prevent Vindya from taking part in labourious work but Vindya won her heart by working tirelessly and efficiently without a murmur. Even the other women of the village were amazed at her qualities.

But, the consequences of this were not quite desirable. The reason being, perhaps that the laws of this world are not exactly as simple as the dictates prescribed in the *'Nitibodh Pratham Bhag'*† written in refined language. A cruel and sarcastic devil seemed to

---

* a kind of wooden chariot carried by four bearers on shoulders usually a bride sits in a palki after wedding

† Nitibodh Pratham Bhag: A moralestic text written to reform society (first part)

have entered somewhere in between all these straightforward rules and laws and entangled them furiously. Thus it is that good work does not always bring about good consequences, sometimes complicating simple matters.

Anathbandhu had two younger and an elder brother. The elder brother earned a meagre fifty rupees and stayed far from home. This would provide for the entire family and fund for the education of the younger brother.

Needless to say that fifty rupees a month is not at all sufficient to run a family well in today's scenario, but it was definitely enough to boost the ego of the elder brother's wife Shyamasundari. Her husband worked the whole year and thus his wife seemed to have acquired the right to a full year of leisure. She never stirred an inch but behaved in such a way that it seemed that just by being the wife of a man who was capable of earning an income she had greatly obliged the entire family.

When Vindyavasini made an entry into this scene and dedicated herself totally to housework day and night, Shyamasundari's narrow mind seemed to tighten like a spring and recoil. It was difficult to guess the reason. Perhaps the elder daughter-in-law had thought that *'Mejobou'** or Vindyavasini had wilfully indulged in lowly housework even though she was from an affluent household just to show how capable she herself was and in the process had shamed her elder sister-in-law. Whatever it might have been somehow, the fifty rupees-a-month wife could not see eye-to-eye with this girl from a rich family. She saw traces of inherent pride in Vindya's modest nature.

---
* second daughter-in-law of a household

On the other hand, Anathbandhu established a library after coming back to the village; got together some twenty school boys and being their president began sending telegrams to newspapers. He even acted as a special correspondent for a few English newspapers and astounded the villagers. But he failed to bring a penny home. On the other hand he spent extravagantly outside.

Vindyavasini would goad him all the time to take up any kind of job. But he did not pay any heed to her words. He told his wife that there were quite a few suitable jobs for him but the partial British government only appointed influential British officials for those posts. A Bengali could never hope to be considered even if he was immensely suitable.

Shyamashankari began to aim poisonous verbal arrows regularly at her brother-in-law and his wife sometimes directly; sometimes indirectly. She would often boast of their own penury saying, "We are poor; how can we maintain a rich man's daughter and son-in-law? They were living quite well over there with no kind of trouble—now how would they bear to live here with only rice and pulses to eat!"

The mother-in-law was in awe of her elder daughter-in-law. So she did not dare to take the side of the weaker opponent. And so did the 'Mejobou' of this family. She tolerated living on the monthly fifty rupees earned meagre meals and bore the earner's wife's daily verbal assaults patiently.

In the meantime, the elder brother returned for a few days on leave and heard a series of enthusiastic narrations from his wife every night. Ultimately when interrupted sleep became a regular feature every night and grew quite serious, he called Anathbandhu and told him calmly and affectionately, "You should try to secure a job, how long can I manage the household alone?"

Anathbandhu roared like a trampled snake, "I cannot tolerate such torture just for two fists of inferior quality rice served two times a day". He immediately decided to go back to his in-laws's house with his wife. But his wife did not agree at all. According to her, the younger brother of a family had an inherent right to share the elder brother's food and were also privileged to bear the harsh words of the elder sister-in-law. But to take shelter with one's father-in-law was utterly shameful. Vindyavasini was prepared to live with a low self-esteem in her in-laws house but she wished to move around her own father's place with her self-esteem intact and a head held high.

Just at this juncture, there arose a vacancy for the third master's post in the local entrance school. Both Anathbandhu's brother and Vindyavasini began to coax him to join the job. Even this plan back fired. When he heard that his own brother and one and only better half was considering him eligible for such a terribly mean job, he was gravely hurt and lost interest in the world and all kinds of activities associated with it even further.

Then again his brother caught hold of his hands and pleaded with him to cool down. All of them thought, it would be wise to leave him alone, as long as he stayed there it would be good for the family.

The elder brother left for his workplace after the short leave came to an end. Shyamashankari put on a big face in suppressed vengeance which made it appear like an ugly, huge, round wheel. Anathbandhu told Vindyavasini, "Nowadays you do not get a decent job unless you go abroad. I have decided to do so—you must organise some money from your father on some pretext or other!"

On hearing his plans to go abroad Vindya was thunderstruck. The thought of going to her father to ask for the money was quite unacceptable to her. She died of shame just thinking about it.

Anathbandhu's bloated ego prevented him from asking for the money from his father-in-law; but he failed to comprehend why a daughter hesitated to secure the amount from her father either by trickery or by coercion. He rebuked his wife on this issue and the grieved Vindhhyavasini had to shed a volley of tears.

A few days passed in utter penury and mental anguish. Ultimately *Durgapuja** in the season of 'Sarat' drew near. Rajkumar Babu sent a bevy of vehicles to welcome his daughter and son-in-law home with open arms and arranged for it in great splendour. After almost a year, the daughter along with her husband entered her father's place once again. The son-in-law was treated with utmost care this time—much much more than the other affluent relative a fact which had deeply hurt the son-in-law earlier.

Even Vindyavasini could take off her veil and enjoy the affectionate indulgences of her near and dear ones and get swept off in the mad wave of festivities after a pretty long time.

Today was Sashti, the beginning of the Pujas. Tomorrow it was to be the 'Saptamipuja'. There was no end to the noise and commotion. All the rooms of

---

* *Durgapuja* takes place on five days—Sashti, Saptami, Ashtami, Navami, Dasami consecutively. An important big festival to worship Goddess Durga generally held in the autumn months. Durga is the embodiment of heavenly power winning over the demon 'Mahisasura' symbolising evil

the palatial building was full to the brim with relations and friends both close and distant.

That night a weary Vindyavasini lay on the bed. This room was not the one where she would sleep earlier. This time her mother had vacated her own bedroom to accommodate her son-in-law just to show extra concern. Vindyavasini did not even know when Anathbandhu went to bed. She was in deep slumber then.

The *shehnai* began to play from early morning. But the weary Vindyavasini did not wake up. Her two friends Kamal and Bhuvan tried to overhear through the bedroom door to no avail and gave up trying jesting laughing loudly from outside. Vindya woke up in a huff and found that her husband was not in bed! She had not known when he had left the room. Embarrassed, she climbed down from the bed only to find her 'mother's very own ironchest open and the cash box which her father would keep inside also missing.

Then she remembered, last evening there had been quite a commotion in the household as her mother's bunch of keys could not be found anywhere. There was no doubt that a thief had stolen the keys with this intention. Then again she was afraid that that thief had hurt her husband in some way. Her heart skipped a beat. As she searched underneath the bed, she saw a letter lying there with the key bunch on top near the leg of the cot.

The letter was in her husband's handwriting. She opened it only to know that her husband had somehow organised the shipping fare for going abroad through a friend; but as he did not have any other means of living there he had no other option but to rob his father-in-law last night. Thereafter he had escaped by the wooden stairs adjoining the balcony fleeing through the garden in the interiors and then crossing over the boundary wall. His ship had left this morning.

Vindyavasini blood curled within as she read the letter. She slumped down that instant catching hold of the pillars of the cot. A death-like murmuring sound almost like the droning of crickets seemed to ring within her entire being beating against her ear drums oblivious to any other sound. Overlapping this tumult within her, several *shehnais* began to play from the courtyard and the neighbouring houses. It appeared as if the whole country was steeped in joy and revelry.

The sunshine of a bright, festive and joyous 'Sarat' morning entered gleefully into the bedroom. On finding the door shut till so late that too on a festive day, the two girls Bhuvan and Kamal jovially and laughing out began to beat upon the door loudly. But when they still did not elicit any reply from within slightly afraid they cried out, "Bindi' 'Bindi!" in a loud voice.

Vindyavasini said in a choked voice "I'm coming, you may go now."

Fearing that she was ailing, the girls ran to call her mother. The mother asked her, "Bindu dear, what has happened? Why is the door bolted even now?" Bindi controlled her tears and said, "Please bring *Baba** here."

The mother, terribly anxious, immediately brought Rajkumar Babu to the door. Vindya opened the door and drawing both of them inside, quickly bolted the door once again.

Then Vindya fell on her knees and catching hold of her father's feet cried out in a heart-rending voice,

---

* father in Bengali families is called 'Baba'

"Baba! Please forgive me, I have stolen money from your chest."

They slumped on the bed in utter surprise. Vindya thereafter explained that she had committed this theft only to help her husband to go abroad.

When her father asked, "Why didn't you ask for the money?" Vindya replied, "So that you would not prevent him from going abroad."

Rajkumar Babu was extremely angered. The mother cried and so did the daughter. All along a joyful music kept on playing from all around the city of Calcutta in strange tunes. That Vindya who had refused to ask her father for money and who could do her utmost to hide any trace of dishonour which her husband might have suffered in the eyes of her own kith and kin, was now totally destroyed. Amidst all the people and the revelry all around, her pride as a wife, her respect as a daughter her self-respect everything that she held dear just broke into pieces and like the dust raised by the feet of her own people (known and unknown) lay accumulated on the floor.

The whole household full to the brim with guests and relatives was abuzz with the shameful story of how Anathbandhu had fled abroad after conspiring with his wife and how he had stolen the key and robbed the money from the family safe overnight. Bhuvan, Kamal and many other relatives and neighbours as well as servants overheard this conversation standing at the doorstep. All of them had assembled there absorbed by curiousity and anxiety as they had seen their master and mistress entering their son-in-law's bolted room looking worried.

Vindyavasini did not appear in public. She locked thereafter, the door and remained in bed without taking a morsel of food. But no one sympathised with her in her hour of grief. Everyone was amazed at the traitor's audacity.

All of them thought how Vindhya's real character had been concealed from them before as there had been no occasion for knowing her. The auspicious ceremony was somehow performed in this lacklustre household.

III

Vindya returned to her in-laws' place steeped in shame and weary in spirit. Here gradually an intimate bond developed between a widow pained by separation from her son and a wife suffering from the pangs of separation from her husband. Both of them came closer to each other as never before and carried on with the minutest details of housework in a spirit of deep patience. Both of them were under the shadow of a silent grief. Vindya grew as far apart from her own parents as she grew closer and closer to her mother-in-law. Vindhya felt, "My mother-in-law is not affluent, neither am I, and thus my parents are far apart from us". Vindya had always felt distant from her parents because of her own poverty. And now she had further fallen in their eyes. Who ever knew whether close, familial ties of affection could bear the burden of such wide differences!

In the first few days Anathbandhu would regularly write letters to his wife. But, slowly letters grew less frequent and gradually a kind of neglect seemed to be felt though, not very pronouncedly expressed.

There were many English women much greater in intelligence, qualifications and beauty than his illiterate wife always busy housekeeping and who considered Anathbandhu a deserving groom both in intelligence and looks. It was not surprising that under such circumstances, Anathbandhu would never consider his simply clad, shrouded and dark-complexioned wife as his equal in any respect.

Inspite of his feelings, he did not hesitate to send a telegraph to this very helpless Bengali girl for money when he really required it. And, it was this very ordinary Bengali girl who sold off all her ornaments to send him the money keeping only a pair of glass bangles for herself. All her valuable jewellery was in safe custody at her father's place as there was no safe place in this village where she could have kept them. But Vindyavasini brought them one by one on the pretext of going for invitations on more than one occasion. Ultimately, after selling off her gold armlets, silver bangles, her benarasi sari even her shawl, she wrote to her husband swearing on herself, smudging each word in each line with her tears humbly pleading him to return home.

Her husband returned as a barrister—with hair cut short, clean shaven and dressed in a well-cut suit, and put up, in a hotel. It was quite impossible to stay in his father's place—firstly because there was no suitable accomodation there, and the second was that the poor, middle-class villagers would never accept people who had become *outcaste*.* His in-laws were rigidly orthodox Hindus, hence they too would not give him shelter.

---

* people who have lived with non-Hindu foreigners were considered to be outcaste in society

Very soon, he ran out of money and had to rent a house instead of staying in a hotel. But he was not prepared to bring his wife there. After returning from abroad, he had visited his wife and mother only two times and had not met them thereafter.

These two grief-stricken women had only one consolation and that was that Anathbandhu was now in his own country and living not very far away, from his near and dear ones. Moreover their pride at Anathbandhu's extraordinary achievements as a barrister knew no bounds. Vindyavasini had been till now the undeserving wife of a famous husband. But the other hand, she could feel this pride in her husband because she considered herself undeserving. She was subdued by grief and swollen by pride both at the same time. She despised Western culture, but even then looked up to her husband and thought, "Nowadays a great many people are turning into a *'Saheb'** but does anyone of them look like him? He is just like a full-fledged 'Saheb'. Whoever says that he is a Bengali!"

When he could bear his living expenses no longer, Anathbandhu decided in despair that in this blessed India there was no room for excellence; where even his colleagues in business were secretly trying to create obstacles in his path out of sheer jealousy, or when the vegetarian items on his plate grew more than the non-vegetarian ones; when fried prawns began to usurp the honourable position of roasted chicken in his food; when the glamour of his clothes and his clean-shaven face began to shed off some of its illuminating glory; or when the highly strung strings of his life seemed to gradually come down to a sad base tune just then a severe accident happened in the lives of the family of Rajkumar Babu

---

* a suave Western gentleman

which brought about a serious change in the trouble prone life of Anathbandhu. Once, while returning by boat from his maternal uncle who lived close to the Ganges river, Harakumar, the only son of Rajkumar Babu was drowned along with his wife and young son when his boat clashed with a steamer on the way. This tragic incident left Vindyavasini as the only surviving member in the family of Rajkumar.

After the terrible grief had somewhat subsided, Rajkumar Babu requested Anathbandhu in pleading tones, "Baba, you go through a ceremony of *penance** to be considered in our caste once again. I do not have anyone else in my family now."

Anathbandhu agreed to this proposal with eagerness. He thought the other barristers who frequented the bar-libraries working with him envied him and did not bother to show due respect towards his extraordinary intellect, he could in this way take revenge.

Rajkumar Babu heeded to the advice of the wise pundits. They ordained that if Anathbandhu had not consumed beef yet he could be enunciated into the higher caste easily.

Even though this four-footed forbidden category of food had been prominent in his list of favourite eatables abroad; Anathbandhu did not hesitate to deny the same. He sarcastically told his dear friends, "When the society wishes deliberately to hear falsehood, I do not see why I should not gratify their wish by just a verbal assurance. Our modern society has a rule that the tongue which has tasted beef should be 'purged' by two ugly

---

* practice of 'penance' or 'purging out of sin'. Arises from the early Hindu custom of enunciation of a person who had deviated from some specific principles of caste and religion

substances like cowdung and falsehood to purify it, and I do not wish to deviate from this norm".

An auspicious date was fixed for the 'penance' ceremony to elevate him to his former position in society. In the meantime not only did Anathbandhu switch over to *dhoti** and chaddar†, he engaged in advice and debated for and against both the Western wise and the Hindu social order. Whoever heard him was immensely pleased with his wisdom.

The affectionate and soft heart of Vindyavasini began to leap with joy and pride. She told herself "Whoever returns from abroad is transformed totally into an Englishman. No one can even recognise him as a Bengali. But my husband has returned absolutely untarnished. On the otherhand, his faith in the Hindu religion seemed to have grown tenfold."

Rajkumar Babu's room was crowded by a bevy of Brahmin pandits on the appointed day. There was no limit to the money spent on the arrangements. There was adequate food for them and care was taken to give them a deserving send-off.

There were no bounds to ceremony even in the interiors of the household. The entire mansion and the courtyard was resounding with the care and hospitality rendered for the invitees. Amidst this terrible commotion and an ocean of formal duties Vindyavasini was moving around in utmost joy just as a light cloud floats in the sky brightened by the 'Sarat' sunlight driven around by the morning breeze. The main protagonist of today's huge worldly drama was, undoubtedly her husband. It

---

* a white piece of cotton cloth worn by men tied in a special way around the waist

† a shawl over the shoulders. These two complete the essemble of an Indian gentleman

appeared as if the entire state was assembled upon a single stage and once the curtain was drawn only Anathbandhu would be exhibited before the curious eyes of a worldly audience. Here 'penance' was not a confession of crime, it was as if he was showing mercy upon them all. It somehow appeared that by coming back and by stepping into the society of the Hindus had glorified it further. And, now that glory of his had reflected its light all around the country, its manifold rays had been scattered everywhere and was now being radiated in the gay, loving face of Vindyavasini in a beautiful, illuminating shade. All the sorrow and mean ignominy of her insignificant life which she had carried all along had been dispelled and she was now seated in the throne of glory with her head held high looking down on all her relatives crowded around in her father's place. The nobility of her husband had transformed a plain, uncouth wife into a respectable citizen of the world.

The ceremony had just ended. Anathbandhu had been elevated to his former caste once again. The invitees, relations and Brahmins had sat along with him and just finished their meals with satisfaction.

The relations called for the son-in-law indoors. The son-in-law in casual spirits, chewing the betel leaf with a happy smile on his face went indoors with his long shawl touching the floor as he walked in slow, stealthy, casual footsteps.

The Brahmins while waiting in the hall for their 'dakshina' after a full lunch were now deeply engrossed in an enlightened, heated discussion. The master of the house, Rajkumar Babu was resting for a while listening to the loud arguments on the '*Smritis*'* seated in an

---

* religious laws set down by wisemen

august gathering. In the meantime the guard came to hand him a card and announced, "A foreign lady has arrived."

Rajkumar Babu was startled. The next moment he glanced at the card to see the name scribed in English. It said—Mrs Anathbandhu Sarkar. Which meant, the 'wife' of Anathbandhu!

Rajkumar Babu could not fathom out the meaning of these simple words even after closely examining them for quite some time. At that moment the newly arrived, pink-cheeked, blonde, blue-eyed, snow-white, English lady stepped into the room herself with deer-like movements and stood in the centre of the hall examining the faces of all the people seated there. But she could not spot the dear face she knew so well. On her entry all of a sudden the heated discussion on the Vedas came to a standstill and the meeting ground assumed the silence of a graveyard.

At that very moment Anathbandhu with his hanging shawl and slow, sweeping movements entered the dramatic scene once more. And, within second, the English lady ran to embrace him and planted a kiss on his betel-stained lips as a gesture of wedded reunion.

Discussions on the 'Samriti' could not be resumed in the meeting hall any further that afternoon.

November-December 1301

✭✭✭✭✭

Eight

The Judge
Bicharak

I

When at long last a middle-aged, not so young Khiroda found the shelter of a man after going through a series of changing partners, she had never dreamt that he too would forsake her like one discards old, worn out clothes. She now felt terribly ashamed to search for another person who would shelter her and provide her with a morsel of food.

There comes a time in life soon after youth which, like the pure white season of *Sarat**, is deep, calm and maturely beautiful—the time for the fruition and the reaping of the crop of life. It does not somehow match with the reckless nature of youth one exhibits in the spring of life. By this time we have finished building our homes amidst this rushing world; a series of good and bad times, a fair number of joys and sorrows have blended together and mellowed and matured the inner being of us all. By now we have somehow succeeded in bringing back all our desires from the past—a magical, imaginary world built up of impossible dreams beyond our reach—into our very own, insignificant abodes within our own prescribed limits—now one cannot

---

* Season in September-October close to Autumn in the West signifying the fall

attract the lovelorn glances in the first pangs of love, but one becomes dearer to the ones with whom one lives. Then the glamour in youth gradually begins to fade, but the ageless, innermost nature of a person seems to etch itself out clearly on one's features through living together for years together—that very smile, look or voice is influenced by that innermost being. It is that time when one does not care much for what has not been received, stops mourning for those who have forsaken him, forgives those who have cheated. Instead one derives a sense of satisfaction and the fruition of all worldly efforts from drawing near all those who have loved and been with one, those few who have been left behind not withstanding all worldly turbulences, sorrows and separations thus creating a secure nest within this certain, testified, eternally well-known circle of loved near and dear ones. There can be no one more unfortunate than one who in the mellowed evening of youth, in this peaceful stage of one's life has to still carry on a futile search for a new identity or a new worldly tie—one for whom no bed awaits nor is any evening lamp lit in anticipation of return.

When Khiroda—touching the limits of her youth—woke up early one morning to find that her lover had escaped with all her ornaments and money the night before; and that she had no means left to pay the house rent or to pay for the milk required for her three-year old son she began to think about herself. When she thought, she had not been able to bind a single man with love in her thirty-eight years of life, had not even secured the right to live and die in the four walls of a secure home; when she remembered that today once again she would have to wipe out her tears and wear colour in her eyes, paint her lips red and rouge her cheeks, when she would have to mesmerise with strange guiles thus covering up her worn out youth and spread the webs of feminine charm once again to win a new heart—all with a smile and unlimited forbearing, she could not bear it any longer. Bolting the door, she lay on the floor and kept banging her head on its hard surface and remained hungry and listless the entire day. Evening set in. Darkness began to descend in the corner of this lampless home. By chance, an old lover of hers had arrived just then. He knocked on the door crying out, 'Khiro, Khiro!' At this, suddenly Khiroda opened the door and burst onto the scene, broom in hand, roaring aloud like an angry tigress; and the lusty young man did not know which way to run.

The boy, unable to bear the pangs of hunger, had cried himself to sleep below the cot. He woke up at this sudden commotion and, in the darkness cried out 'Ma Ma' in a voice laden with tears.

At this moment Khiroda caught hold of the child tightly to her chest, ran at lightning speed and jumped into the nearby well.

Hearing the loud thump, neighbours arrived with lamps in their hands. It was not long before Khiroda and the child were picked up from the well. Khiroda was unconscious but the child had died by then.

Khiroda recovered in the hospital. The magistrate ordered that she be kept in the sessions court on charges of murder.

II

Our judge Mohitmohan Dutta is a statutory civilian. His iron judgement ordained that Khiroda be hanged to death. Considering her pitiable condition, the lawyers tried their best to save this hapless woman but failed to succeed. The judge did not think that she deserved a bit of mercy.

There were reasons for this. On one hand, he addressed Hindu women as *Devis**, but on the other he possessed extreme disbelief against them. He was of the opinion that, women were always inclined to rip open the bonds of society and family and if at any time, rules and restrictions were given a free rein, there would not be a single good lady left in the cages of this social structure.

There was also another reason behind this belief of his. To know that we have to discuss a part of the history of Mohit's young days.

When Mohit was a college student in the second year, he was radically different from his present stature both in looks and behaviour. Now Mohit sports a bald head and a *tiki*† on the back of it and his face is cleanshaven every morning, but those days he looked more like a new edition of *Kartika*‡ of the nineteenth century with his Western hairstyle, golden "spectacles", beard and a moustache. He gave special attention to clothes and bore no indifference towards alcohol and its paraphernalia. Moreover, he had some co-related interests too.

A family lived in a house not far away. They had a widowed daughter named Hemshashi. She would not be more than fourteen or fifteen.

---

* A Goddess in Bengali mythology
†A strand of hair at the back of a bald head showing that the man is a Brahmi
‡ Signifying charm and good looks, son of Goddess Durga and a bachelor God in Hindu mythology

A green, densely foliaged seashore might appear wonderfully dreamy and picture perfect when seen from mid-ocean but does not remain so when one actually reaches the bank. Fettered by the chains of widowhood, the world of which she had been deprived would appear to Hemshashi like an eternally distant, deeply mysterious, intensely pleasurable forbidden territory. She did not know that the machinery of this worldly industry was immensely complicated and steel-hard—an incomprehensible admixture of joy and sorrow, prosperous well-being and dangerous situations, uncertainty and crisis, frustration and regret. She would think the course of life ran smoothly like the clear waters of a bubbling stream, all the roads and ways of this beautiful world ahead were gateways to heaven, happiness was waiting for her a step away and unfulfilled desire was stored only in the pulsating, woeful, soft heart of hers hidden inside the ribs of her chest. Especially then, when, from the distant horizon of the skies of her inner being, the pulsating winds of youth had coloured the entire world before her in strange hues of spring, the vast blue sky had been filled to the brim with the flowing waves of her youthful heart, and the world appeared to have blossomed into several layers of soft, red lotus petals all around the fragrant cells of her young heart.

She had no one at home besides her parent and two younger brothers. The two brothers would have their meals and leave for school quite early, come back from school and after the evening supper leave for study in the local night school. The father's salary was meagre—he could not afford to keep a tutor at home.

In her leisure hours, Hem would sit at the window of her lonely room. She would gaze unflinchingly at the traffic movements on the main road. The travelling salesman would call out loudly in a sad tone. She would listen and think how happy the travellers were—even the beggars were so independent, and the salesman too seemed earning a living quite easily; to her they appeared as great actors acting out their respective roles in this pulsating population's happy dramatic enactment.

And, she could also observe the well-dressed, conceited and broad-shouldered Mohitmohan at all times of the day. She would imagine he looked like the greatest of all mankind blessed with good fortune in every possible way, almost like the *Lord Mahendra**. She would feel that erect, well-dressed, handsome young man possessed all the good qualities in this world and she could give him all that was her own. This young widow would form a mental image of Mohit putting together all kinds of glorious attributes and worship him as a God very similar to a girl playing with a doll imagining it to be a live person.

On some evenings she would see Mohit's room lit up with bright lights and hear the ringing of anklets of some female dancer and songs being rendered in a female voice. On nights like these she would stay awake staring longingly at the fickle, swiftly moving shadows on the wall. Her aggrieved, ailing heart would beat upon her ribs in terrible anguish.

Did she blame or chide her fake god for this extravagance in her heart of hearts? No, never. The brightly lit room troubled by the loud orchestra echoing with an unbridled excess of luxury would attract Hemshashi as a distant mirage just as fire attracts flies tempting them with dreams of a star studded sky.

---

*Lord Shiva also known as such in Hindu mythology symbolising a combination of rare qualities in a man

She would sit alone in the darkness of the night and create a magical world from the lights, the shadow and the music visible to her through the far-away window and add her own desires and imagination to it. Then, she would install her mental idol amidst this illusory kingdom and gaze at it in wonder and adulation. She would light up her entire existence and youth, personal joys and sorrows, this life and the next like an incense stick lit in the flames of desire and worship him in this isolated, silent temple of her heart. Little did she know that the waves of extravagance which were flowing behind that wall contained terrible weariness, inconsolable guilt, murkiness, terrifying lust and inflammable fire. The widow could not make out from a distance how a heartless cruelty snarling a wicked smile remained hidden inside that sleepless, magically lit night life she so coveted from afar.

She could have spent her entire life in her dream-like trance sitting at her own, isolated window weaving a world around this heavenly dream and conjured images of a god-like figure. But, unfortunately for her, God took pity on her and the heavens for which she craved grew closer. But when heaven comes closer to earth and touches it, not only do the heavens crash down, the person who had created it in her loneliness too breaks into several pieces scattering on the ground.

We need not go into details on when Mohit cast his lustful eye on this devoted girl at the window, or when he wrote frequent letters to her signing them as 'Vinodchandra'—a fictitious name, or how he at last received a reply written in a fearful and hesitant tone full of spelling errors yet brimming with emotions. Or how, thereafter, a storm seemed to brew what with the queries and replies, joy and shy hesitation, suspicion and respect, hope and apprehension, and how then, the entire world had appeared to circle around the widow in a destructive, intense desire for happiness and thus circling, was wiped out by itself into a pointless shadow. How this woman ultimately one day leaped out of this circling web of worldly existence and was thrown out far, far away is a story I do not consider necessary to elaborate.

In the darkness of a night, Hemshashi abandoned her parents, brothers and home and sat with Mohit whom she knew as Vinodchandra in a closed carriage. When the idol whom she had worshipped from afar sat closely to her shedding off all his godly aura; she was suddenly overcome with shame and regret.

When at last the carriage began to move, she fell on Mohit's feet crying and said, "I beg you, please let me go home". Startled at this, Mohit covered her mouth, and the carriage began to move at a fast pace.

Just as a drowning man remembers all the events of his life in a single moment, Hemshashi too, in the deep darkness of the shut carriage remembered how her father would not eat his meal unless she sat there in front of him, how her youngest brother loved to be fed by his eldest sister after he came back from school. She also remembered how she would dress the betel leaf along with her mother in the morning and how her mother would tie her hair in the evening.

Every small corner of the house and every little household duty sparkled brightly on her mind's eye. She now felt that her lonely life and small little home was heaven itself. That betel leaf preparation, hair dressing, fanning her father when he sat down for dinner, plucking out his grey hair when he rested on holidays in the afternoon, tolerating the pranks of her younger brothers—all of these seemed greatly peaceful and valuable to her now. She could not figure out whether there was a need to be happy in some other way when all these reasons for happiness were already present.

She remembered how all the other girls from good families were now lost in deep slumber in their secure little homes in this wide, unknown world. Why did she fail to comprehend how pleasurable it was to sleep peacefully on one's own bed in one's own room! Those good girls would wake up the next morning in their respective rooms and engage in their regular everyday duties with no guilt or remorse in their hearts. But homeless Hemshashi did not know where her sleepless night would end—how in that joyless morning of hers the well-known, quiet yet pleasant sun rays would fall on their small little household at the corner of a narrow lane revealing sudden shame and ignominy! What terrible humiliation and suffering would then occur!

Hem cried her heart out and pleaded in a sad manner, "There is still time. Please reach me home before my mother and two brothers wake up." But, her idol did not heed her request. He had pulled her into a second-rate noisy-wheeled chariot and was now taking her to the heavenly world she had long desired.

After a short interval from now, the 'god' and the 'heaven' he had promised took recourse to another second-rate, worn out carriage and went the other way round—the woman was left behind immersed in neck-deep remorse.

III

I have quoted only, one specific incident from Mohitmohan's past history. I have not yet mentioned many other such incidents so that this narrative does not get too 'repetitive'.

Now, there is really no need to rake in bygone matters. No one would perhaps, even remember the name 'Vinodchandra' today. Mohit has turned into a new leaf—he performs rites of worship religiously and regularly discusses the scriptures. He is keenly undertaking yoga practices for small children and strictly prohibiting the women of the house from exhibiting themselves keeping them confined to the interiors where even the sun, moon and the other planets can not intrude. But, today, perhaps because he had crimed against several women, he is extra firm about ordering capital punishment for women who have committed any social crimes.

Two or three days after giving the verdict on Khiroda, food-lover Mohit had gone to collect some select vegetables from the jail garden. He was curious to know whether Khiroda was now repentant for her 'fallen' lifestyle and the crime she had committed. He entered the women's cell.

He could hear a loud quarrel somewhere in the distance. He entered the room to find Khiroda engaged in a terrible quarrel with the guard. Mohit smiled to himself—"This is what makes a woman! Death knocking at the door but she still has to quarrel! Perhaps this species will fight even with the messenger of death once they reach *Yamalaya*"*.

---

* Lord of Death. His abode is known as Yamalaya or heaven and his messenger is called Yamadoot in Hindu mythology

Mohit thought, even now she should be repentant for her actions and he could do that with some gentle rebuke and some good advice. With this noble aim, as he went closer to Khiroda she cried out pleading him, "Oh! Judge babu, I beg of you! Please tell him to return my ring."

He came to know that there had been a ring hidden in her hair and by chance the guard had spotted it and taken it away.

Mohit again smiled to himself "Tomorrow she would step into the gallows; but she has not been able to forget that ring of hers—ornaments seem to be all and end all for all women!"

He called out to the guard, "Here show me the ring." The guard handed him the ring.

He flinched as if he had caught a piece of burning charcoal. On the ring was engraved a small picture of a moustached and bearded young man painted in oil upon an ivory plate and on the other side etched in gold was a name, "Vinodchandra!"

At last, Mohit looked up from the ring and glanced fully into Khiroda's face. He remembered another tearful, loving, delicate, shyly anxious face he had seen twenty-four years back. This face carried some resemblance with that other.

Mohit looked at the ring once again and now when he slowly looked up, the sinner and the fallen woman appeared noble and glorious. The tiny gold ring's unblemished, sparkling brightness looked somewhat like the golden idol of a Goddess!!

January 1301

✮✮✮✮✮

Nine

Humbling of Ego
Darpaharan

I have only recently learnt how to compose a story. No, I have not gained this insight from reading Bankim Chandra* or Sir Walter Scott. In this my first venture of story telling, I will tell you how I learnt this art and from where.

My father did hold some different views, but he had not built up a definite opinion opposing the system of child-marriage, neither from his books nor independent thinking. When I was married I had just completed seventeen and stepped into eighteen. It was the third year of college, and the first flushes of youth had begun to sweep my routine life with innumerable, unfathomable kinds of music and essences from so many invisible directions, breathing and murmuring through my eager self that my heart fills with deep sighs whenever I remember it even today.

My mother was not alive, and my father brought in this twelve-year-old girl Nirjharini† to fulfil the void created by her absence without waiting for me to complete my studies.

I hesitate to suddenly spell out the name 'Nirjharini', to my readers, since most of them must be quite grown-up—some schoolmasters, some *munsifs*‡, and some

---

* a judicial officer
† famous writer and novelist in Bengali
‡ a name meaning 'stream' or river

engaged in editing. I fear that they would laugh at my father-in-law's taste in selection of names and the extremity of grace and novelty of it all. But I was ignorant then, and had no problems of logical thinking. Thus when I first heard this name as the marriage alliance was being arranged, I felt as if the word entered my heart through my ears and made me mad. Now I am older and very keen to become a *munsif* from a lawyer, but that name still rings in my heart like the musical notes of an old violin and seems to grow softer by the years.

The first love of early years is sweeter because of so many small hindrances. The hindrances of shame, of people at home, of inexperience, and the rays which throw light from behind these obstacles are as colourful as the early morning rays—they are not as clear, naked and colourless as the afternoon sunlight.

My father came between our newly acquired relationship like the Vindhya hills. He banished me to a hostel and strove to teach his daughter-in-law reading and writing in the Bengali language. My story begins from there.

My father-in-law was not to be outdone—not only did he name his daughter, he had arranged for her education as well. She had even learnt to read the scriptures by heart. She did not even need to read the footnotes given by Hembabu* whilst reading the *Meghnadvadh Kavya*†.

I had come to know of her prowess in the language only after I went back to the hostel. I somehow, through various intricacies, secretly contrived to write some

---

* writer in contemporary Bengal
† epicwritten by Michael Madusudhan Dutt, renowned poet of Bengal—a landmark in history of Bengali literature

heavy, emotionally charged letters to her, much to the ignorance of my father. In one of these letters, I had quoted several selected couplets from the works of our modern poets but without marking them with the right quote marks. I had thought it wasn't enough just to attract the affections of my beloved, her love for me should be based on respect, I did not naturally possess that style in Bengali which could draw her respect.

My letter could only string together the gems which had been pierced by other expert jewellers. But I had not thought it wise enough to announce with utmost modesty that the jewels which constituted this product were the works of someone else and only the string was mine. Even the great Kalidas would not have done so, if truly these jewels had been usurped from elsewhere.

However, after I received her reply, I did not resist myself any more from marking the quotation signs wherever necessary. It was understood that the new bride was well-versed in the Bengali language. I was not the right judge to find out whether her letter contained errors in spelling—but I could guess that no one could have written such a letter until and unless she possessed a literary sensibility and a powerful grasp over the language.

It would be grossly unfair to blame me for not having felt some pride and joy at my wife's abilities as any other husband would, but that was shadowed by a different kind of feeling. That feeling might not have been of impeccable standards, but it sure was normal. The trouble was that the way in which I could have introduced my own abilities would be tough for this young girl to comprehend with her limited English, sending her a model of writing based on Burke Macaulay's style of letter writing would be like firing on a tiny mosquito—the insect would not perish, but the atmosphere would be polluted by smoke and commotion.

I could not resist showing off my wife's letters to three of my bosom friends. They marvelled and said, "It is your good fortune that you have acquired such a wife." That would mean, in an indirect manner, that I was not deserving enough to have such a gifted wife.

I had written a few letters to Nirjharini even before I got her reply.

They were brimming with emotions but also contained plenty of errors in spelling. I had not deemed it necessary then to write more cautiously. If I had done so, the letters would have been literally more correct, but the flood of emotions unleashed would have been abruptly brought to an end.

Amidst such a situation, it was safer to 'love talk' in person, leaving aside communicating through letters. Thus, I had to bunk college whenever my father left for office. We would make up for this loss in our study hours by our hours of intimate conversation perhaps with enhanced interest. I have time and time again tested this scientific theory in the laboratory of love which says that nothing in this world is absolutely lost—that which appears to be a loss could perhaps become a gain in a different form.

Around this time my wife's cousin sister's wedding had been fixed. We had, as was the custom, relieved ourselves of our duties of hosting the *aiburobhat*, a special lunch for the bride.

My wife could not resist herself and had poured all her affections in a poem on a red piece of paper etched out scarlet in ink to send to the bride. Somehow, my

---

* lunch hosted for a bachelor or maiden before the wedding

father got hold of it. He was ecstatic at his newly acquired daughter-in-law's poetry—the excellent composition, clarity of thought, beauty of expression and many other qualities approved by literary experts astounded him. He exhibited it to his aged friends, and they agreed with him. They puffed on their tobacco pipes and commented, "Excellent!" That my wife possessed a considerable amount of literary prowess became an open secret. This new composer's cheeks and ear tips turned a shade of crimson at this sudden outburst of fame, but with time she evolved out of her shyness. As I have said before, nothing in this world ever ends—perhaps traces of that shame had left her cheeks and taken shelter in some hidden crevice of my own stone-heart.

But I did not leave anything undone in the duties of a husband. I had never shown any lethargy in correcting errors in her composition through my wise, impartial criticism.

The more my father gave her his unstinted encouragement, I doubled the effort by cautiously pointing out the defects in her writing to bring the required balance in her nature. I did all that I could to deter her, showed her the works of famous authors of English literature, thereby astounding her. She had written a few lines on a cuckoo but I subdued her enthusiasm by reading out Shelley's poem on a skylark and Keats' lines on a nightingale. I felt I too had participated in the glory of Shelley and Keats on account of my widespread knowledge. My wife too would insist on my reading out selected portions from English classics, and I would oblige her with pride. Had I then not overshadowed the intellect of my wife through borrowed brilliance from the glory of English literature?

My father and friends did not realise that a woman's vulnerability needed this much of a shadowed cover protection, and I had to take up this solemn duty. One could laud the appearance of the night moon in the form of the afternoon sun for a while, but then one had to think next how one should suppress its brilliance.

My father along with others had attempted to publish my wife's writings in newspapers. Nirjharini would express embarrassment at this, and I protected her. I did not allow her articles to be published, but could not hinder their circulation amongst friends and associates.

I could fathom the ill effects of such publicity only after some time. I was a lawyer practising in the Alipore High Court by then. Once I was fighting as the prosecution lawyer with full force in a will case. The will had been written in Bengali. I was trying to prove the legal significance of the will in favour of my party when suddenly the defence lawyer spoke aloud, "If only my learned friend had been tutored by his learned wife on what this will really conveyed, perhaps he would not have pained the mother tongue through such strange explanation".

One has to go through extremes when blowing the fire while lighting the oven, but the fire which destroys a home is perhaps inextinguishable. All good words spoken about a person will be buried in oblivion, but the harmful ones spread from mouth to mouth like the flow of wild western wind.

This incident too received wide publicity all around. I feared lest it should reach the ears of my wife. Thankfully it had not—at least I had never heard of it from her.

One day I happened to be introduced to a stranger who asked me almost at once, "Are you the husband of

Mrs Nirjharini Devi?" I answered, "I would not like to answer whether I am her husband or not, but she sure is my wife." I do not consider it respectable to be known to the world outside as a 'wife's husband.'

That was not something to be proud of. I had been reminded by another person in not so clear words. As I said before, the cousin sister of my wife had been married some time back. Her husband was a barbaric and wicked man. The tortures he inflicted upon his wife were unbearable. I had discussed this monster's unforgivable acts in public. These had assumed larger proportions and reached the man's ears. Then onwards he had begun his vindictive tirade against me. He would aim at me and tell all and sundry that he had heard of writers writing on their own selves or even on their fathers-in-law, describing different kinds of qualities—high, low, medium and many such. But this was the first time he had heard of someone turning famous on account of his 'wife's' fame—such a wild imagination had not emerged even from a poet!

It was but natural that my wife would feel some pride when people all over spoke about her in such glowing terms. And especially my father, who had this bad habit, he would humorously compare our knowledge of Bengali in the presence of Nirjharini.

Once he said *"Bouma,** why don't you correct the spellings of the letters which Harish writes to me in Bengali? He had written one to me where he has spelt 'Jagadindra' wrongly." On hearing this, my father's *bouma* smiled softly without uttering a word. I too laughed at it as a jest, but truly such remarks are not to be taken seriously at all.

---

* a daughter in law addressed as such by in-law.

It did not take long for me to find out how pride had got the better of my wife. The boys in our locality had set up a club and they had persuaded a reputed Bengali writer to deliver a lecture on the occasion. Another famous person had been requested to be the president, but the latter had pleaded illness and excused himself the night before. Seeing no other alternative, these boys came to me for help. I was quite overjoyed at this sudden show of respect and said, "Well, all right, tell me what is the topic."

They said, "Old and modern Bengali literature."

I said, "That will be just fine, I know both quite well."

The next day I hurried my wife to arrange my breakfast and clothes before going for the meeting. Nirjharini said, "Why dear, why are you so anxious—are you leaving to search for another bride?" I said, "I have you as my bride."

"Then why this rush to dress up impeccably?"

I explained the matter to my wife in detail. But she did not express any joy on hearing this. She suddenly caught hold of my hand anxiously and asked, "Are you mad? No, no, you must never go there."

I said, "I have heard of Rajput women adorning their husbands before sending them to the battlefield, why can't a Bengali woman see her husband off to a lecture meeting at least?"

Nirjharini said, "I would not have worried if the lecture was in English, but—let it be, so many people would come—you are not accustomed—the consequences... ."

Had I not often thought about the consequences? I remembered the song of Rammohan Roy:

"Think of the terrible last day; when—others would speak, and you remain mute."

If the president suddenly becomes mute when he stands up at the end of the lecture, rendered blind, weak-pulsed and frozen at that moment, then what would happen? I could not claim to be of better health than the earlier, whenever I would think of all these inner points.

I summoned all my ego and asked my wife, "Nirjhar, do you think... .?"

My wife interrupted, "I do not think anything—but today I have got a severe headache, I anticipate a spate of fever, surely you cannot leave me today?"

I said, "Now that is something different. Your face sure has turned a shade of crimson."

I did not strive to decipher whether that shade of crimson was the result of shame, thinking of my sorry state at the meeting, or whether it was due to the drowsiness of fever. I was rescued from the grave task of being the president by excusing myself from the club secretary on the pretext of my wife's illness.

Needless to say, my wife recovered very soon. My inner voice began to warn me, saying, "Everything else is fine, but this doubt in your wife's mind regarding your knowledge of Bengali, well, that is not fine. She had decided that she is highly accomplished—one never knows, one fine day she might think of opening a night school inside the mosquito net itself and teach you Bengali."

I answered, "You're right. I must subdue her pride now itself or else it might surpass all limits."

I picked up a quarrel with her that night. I suggested some examples from Pope's epic to explain to her how dangerous little knowledge could be. I further explained that writing devoid of spelling mistakes and grammatical errors need not be the ideal—the real factor was the 'idea' behind it. I coughed a little and added, "You can never find that in a dictionary, you need brains to generate that." I did not elaborate on exactly who possessed such intelligence, but I think my words were not misunderstood. I proclaimed then, "No woman of any country has ever written something worthwhile."

On hearing this, Nirjharini's feminine sensibilities were hurt. She said, "Why can't women write? Are they so inferior?"

I said, "Anger won't get you anywhere. Give one example at least."

Nirjharini answered, "If I had read as much history as you have, I would certainly quote several such examples."

Such words did offer a balm on my wounded ego, but the debate did not end here. I will later describe how the matter finally came to an end.

Uddipana,* a monthly magazine, had announced fifty rupees as award for the best story. We decided both of us would write two stories for the paper to see who would be the lucky one to win.

This was decided the night before. But I began to suffer from all sorts of apprehensions once the morning dawned and my better sense prevailed. But I vowed I will never let go this opportunity—I have to win by hook or by crook. I still had about two months to work upon.

I bought a special word dictionary and collected literature written by the famous Bengali classical novelist, Bankim Chandra. But Bankim's works were better known to my wife than myself. So I had to let go of that noble influence. I began to read a lot many English story books. I ultimately built up a decent plot line after arranging and rearranging several stories. The

---
* a Bengali monthly magazine

plot was excellent, but the problem was that, in no circumstances could such events ever happen in Bengali society. I built up the foundation of the story on Punjab borders of very ancient times, wherein all doubts of the possible and the impossible could be swept aside and my pen could flow unobstructed; passionate love, exuberant courage, violent consequences revolved around my story like the horses of a circus running along in a strange motion.

I could not sleep at night; in the day at lunch time I would absent-mindedly pour the fish curry into the lentil bowl instead of the plate of rice. Seeing me in such a state, Nirjharini pleaded with me, "Promise me, you will not write any story. I admit defeat."

I grew agitated and said, "Do you think I am wondering about the story night and day. It's nothing of that sort. I have to think about my clients. If I had as much leisure as you to imagine poems and stories, I would've been a carefree person".

Whatever it might be, I struggled to build up a story combining English plot line with Sanskrit vocabulary. My conscience began to prick a little when I thought about Nirjhar—poor little dear—she had never read English literature and thus her field of inspiration was so narrow, my competition with her was not really based on equality.

Epilogue

I have sent the piece I wrote. The *Baisakh** issue is supposed to carry the awarded best story. Although I did not have any doubts, my mind grew more and more apprehensive as the hour of reckoning approached.

---

* Bengali month in summer signifies the New Year

At last the *Baisakh* month arrived. One fine day I came home early to learn that the much awaited *Uddipana* had been released and my wife had already laid her hands on it.

I entered my bedroom on tiptoes, peeped into the room and saw my wife burning a book over the fire. The reflection of her face on the wall mirror showed clearly that she had wept profusely before that.

I was overjoyed but at the same time felt some sympathy for her. Oh! Poor dear—her story had not appeared in *Uddipana*. But to be so sorrowful over this simple matter! A woman's ego is hurt for such petty reasons!

I went back silently again. I bought a paper from the *Uddipana* office spending ready cash. I eagerly opened the paper to see whether my story had been published or not.

The index revealed that the award winning story was not *Vikramnarayan*,* the story that I had written; it was *Nanadini* and the writer—hold your breath—it was, oh no! It was Nirjharini Devi!

I do not know whether there was any other Nirjharini in entire Bengal besides my wife. I read the story and discovered it was the life story of the unfortunate cousin of Nirjhar described in detail. It was totally a home truth—the language was simple but the scene uncovered like a picture and touched the heart so much that my eyes filled with tears. There was no doubt left that this Nirjharini was my very own 'Nirjhar'.

Then I sat quietly for a long while, thinking about the burning scene in my bedroom and the pale face of that pained woman.

---

* the story which the narrator wrote

That night I asked my wife, "Nirjhar, where is the notebook containing all your articles?" She said, "Why? What are you going to do with them?"

I said, "I'll send them for printing."

Nirjharini said, "Aa, ha, you need not fool me."

I said, "No I am not fooling you. I will really get them printed."

Nirjharini replied that she did not know where it had disappeared.

I stubbornly resisted "No Nirjhar, it just cannot be. Tell me, where have you kept it?"

Nirjharini said, "Really I do not have it."

I asked "Why? What happened?"

Nirjharini said she had burnt that.

I was shocked and said, "What! When did you burn it?"

To which she replied, "I burnt it today. Don't I know that what I write is rubbish?

People praise them falsely only because a woman has written them."

I have not been able to persuade Nirjhar to write a few lines even after a lot of pleading after this incident.

Yours

Shri Harish Chandra Haldar

The story which has been narrated so far is largely made up. That my husband knows very little Bengali will be clear to anyone reading the story he has narrated so far. What a shame! Should anyone make up such a story about one's own wife?

Yours

Nirjharini Devi

There have been several speculations about the guiles of women in the scriptures and works of our country and others. You will not be cheated if you remember them now. I will not relate who had corrected the style and spellings in my composition, but the discerning reader will surely guess who it was. The wise reader will also be able to discern that the errors which have been detected in the few lines she has written were totally deliberate. She had found out this simple way to prove that her husband was a wise scholar in Bengali and his story was entirely a made-up one. Perhaps this is the reason why Kalidas* has written that women are the wisest.

[In the confession, Nirjharini deliberately commits spelling mistakes to reveal little knowledge of the Bengali tongue only to undermine her own talents and enlarge her husband's].

He knew the female psyche very well. I too have begun to fathom this mystery of Nature only very recently. Perhaps I too would graduate into being a Kalidas in the near future. I find some more resemblance with Kalidas. I have heard how the poet had committed a serious error when he had composed couplets to impress his newly-wed accomplished wife.

This writer too has gone through several such accidents of using wrong words in the wrong context. After considering these facts in depth I am hopeful that I too might face the ultimate consequence which Kalidas had been fortunate enough to receive.

Yours
Harish

---

* great epic poet in Sanskrit who wrote the *Meghnadvadh* epic. The reference is to the emergence of the wisdom of the poet when he is taunted by his intelligent wife on his ignorance

If this story is printed, I will go back to my father's place.

Nirjhar

I too will leave for my in-laws' immediately afterwards.

Shri Harish

✮✮✮✮✮

Ten

The Living and the Dead
Jeebito O Mrito

I

The widowed bride of the *zamindar* of Ranihaat, Sharadashankar's family did not have anyone in her father's family to call her own. Almost all of them had passed away one by one. She did not have someone in her in-laws' family whom she could call her very own either—neither a husband nor a son. The apple of her eye was the youngest son of Sharadashankar—her nephew-in-law. His mother had been seriously ill after the child was born and hence this widowed aunt Kadambini had brought him up. When one brings up the son of someone else the attachment is much more—perhaps because one has no right over him, no social right, only an affectionate claim. But affection cannot produce any legal document to prove its right in an established society and does not care to do so either. It only wants to love its object of affection with more intensity as it is not certain of its existence.

After showering all her pent-up affections on this boy, the widow Kadambini breathed her last instantly on a *Sravana** night. Suddenly for some unknown reason her heartbeat came to a standstill—time ticked

---
* monsoon month of July-August in Bengali calendar

away as usual everywhere in the world, only the clock inside that affectionate, tiny, soft heart stopped ticking.

Four *Brahmin** workers serving the *zamindar* family immediately carried off the dead body without any pomp or show for the last rites so that the police did not come to know of it.

The crematorium of Ranihaat was situated quite far. There was a cottage beside the lake and a huge banyan tree near it. There was nothing else in that huge ground. A river would flow here before but that had dried up. A part of that dry water-path had been dug to build the lake meant for the use of the crematorium. The people of this area considered this lake as the representative of the holy river Ganges†.

After laying the dead body inside the small hut, these four people awaited the arrival of wooden logs to light the funeral pyre. It was becoming so late that two of them, Nitai and Gurucharan, became impatient and went to see what was the reason behind it. Bidhu and Banamali stayed behind with the dead body.

It was a dark *Sravan* a night. The sky was filled with heavy clouds and not a single star was visible. Both of them sat mum inside the hut. One had a matchbox and a lamp tied to his shawl. The damp matchbox did not light after a lot of struggle—the only lantern they had with them had gone off by now.

After keeping quiet for a long time someone said, "Brother, it would be great to smoke a bowlful of tobacco right now. I did not bring anything in a hurry."

The other man said, "I can run along and get all the ingredients very fast."

---

* upper caste in Hindu religion
† ashes of the dead bodies after cremating are immersed in the holy river of Ganges

Bidhu understood Banamali's motive of doing the disappearing act and said, "Oh! Will you? And I would have to be alone over here, is it?"

Again, the conversation subsided. Every five minutes appeared to be like an hour. They began to abuse the ones who had gone for the wood within themselves—they were quite sure by now that the others were sitting, smoking tobacco and chatting in fine comfort somewhere else.

There was no sound anywhere—only a continuous chiring of crickets and the howls of jackals. At this moment it seemed as if the cot carrying the dead body moved a trifle, as if the body had turned to one side.

Bidhu and Banamali began chanting prayers and trembling inside. Suddenly a loud sigh was heard in the dark room. Bidhu and Banamali now ran out of the room with a leap and headed for their village.

After going for about a mile furlong and a half they found their companions returning with lanterns in their hands. They had really gone out to smoke tobacco, did not know anything about wood, but nevertheless gave information that people were breaking trees to get the wood—and they would start their journey very soon. Now Bidhu and Banamali related the events inside the hut. But Nitai and Gurucharan pooh-poohed it in disbelief and chided them severely for forsaking their duty and coming away.

The four of them returned immediately to the hut in the crematorium. But to their chagrin, they found the dead body had disappeared and only the bare cot lay behind.

All of them stared at each other. What if a jackal had taken the body? But there was not a piece of thread left over there. After searching here and there they found recent and small footsteps of a woman on the bit of clay soil just near the doorway of the hut.

Sharadashankar was not a simple man at all and such ghost stories as these would never convince him. Thus the four of them decided, after a lot of discussion, that it would be much better to convey that the cremation had taken place properly.

When the people arrived with wood in the morning they heard that the body had already been cremated as there was some wood stored inside the hut. No one would ever dream of suspecting this explanation as a dead body was not so valuable that anyone would try to steal it.

II

All of us know that life sometimes remains concealed within a body even though outwardly there are no signs to indicate so and often, after a period of time, the apparently dead body comes back to life. Kadambini too had not really died—suddenly for some unknown reason her body had stopped functioning.

When she regained consciousness, she saw a deep darkness everywhere. She found that she was not lying in the usual place she did every night. She cried out, "Didi", but no one answered her cry in the dark. She sat up with a start and remembered that deathbed of hers. That sudden clutch in her heart almost leading to breathlessness. Her elder sister-in-law had been warming milk for her son over the fire in the corner of the room. Kadambini had not been able to bear the pain any longer—she had cried out in a choked voice, "Didi, please bring Khoka to me—I feel as if I am dying." Then everything had become covered in blackness—as if a bottle of ink had fallen over an exercise book—and Kadambini's entire memory and consciousness, all the letters of the worldly dictionary seemed to have become blurred to dissolve into a single one. Whether Khoka had called her *Kakima* for the last time in his sweet loving tone, whether she had collected this last bit of affection from that well-known world of hers while moving on into this eternal, unknown path of death, the widow could not even recollect.

But when a cool, moist breeze blew in from the open door and the croaking of monsoon frogs came floating, she remembered all the rainy days she had spent since childhood in her short little life and felt a closeness with the living world in that one moment. Once when the lightning struck, she could see the lake, the banyan tree, the huge fields and the far-off line of trees in that fraction of a second. She recalled the times she had bathed in this lake on some holy occasions, and also remembered how she had felt the terror of death when she had seen all those corpses in this very crematorium.

She thought now that she had to go back home. But again immediately thought how could she go back when she was not 'living' as that would mean ill luck for the family. "I have been banished from the kingdom of life—I am my own ghost."

If that was not so, then how had she arrived in this lonely crematorium from the secure interiors of Sharadashankar's house at midnight? If her cremation had not yet taken place, then where were the people who would burn her? She remembered her death scene in the lighted home of Sharadashankar and contrasting it with this distant, deserted, dark crematorium where she was alone, she thought, "I am no more of this society of the world—I am terrible, I am evil, I am my own ghost."

As soon as this thought evolved, she felt as if all her worldly ties had been dissociated from all corners. As if now she was strangely powerful and possessed limitless freedom—she could go anywhere and do anything impossible. When this hitherto unknown new realisation came upon her she was seized with insanity and sprung out of the room like a sudden, fierce blow of wind and walked across the dark crematorium; there was no trace of shame nor worry left in her any more.

Her feet grew weary and her body weak. The fields never seemed to end—there were paddy fields too and knee-deep water had accumulated in some places. The chirping of one or two birds was heard from a bamboo forest in some far-away village as slowly dawn broke upon the sky.

It was then that she felt some kind of a fear. She did not know exactly what her new relationship with the living world would be. As long as she was in the fields or in the cremation ground or in the darkness of the rainy night she seemed to have been fearless as if she was in familiar territory. But now in daylight the living world seemed to her to be a terrible place. The living fear the dead and the dead fear the living—both of them live apart on either side of the river of death.

III

Clad in muddy clothes, dazed in a peculiar state of mind and almost out of mind due to sleeplessness, Kadambini looked so very terrible that people would have feared to glance at her and perhaps little boys would have stoned her from a distance. Fortunately a gentleman met her first in her present state of mind.

He asked her "*Ma**, it appears you are from a well-to-do family, where are you going alone and in this condition?"

Kadambini did not reply and looked at him blankly. She could not, at that instant, think of what to answer. That she was still in the living world, that she looked like a lady from a well-to-do family and the very fact that a traveller was asking her that in the midst of a path to a village—everything seemed unintelligible to her.

The traveller further said, "Come *Ma*, I will reach you home; please tell me where you stay."

Kadambini began to contemplate. She could not dare to think of returning to her in-laws and she did not have her own folks. It was now that she remembered her childhood mate Jogamaya.

Although she had no communication with her childhood mate, they would still write letters to each other now and then. Sometimes a real love tiff would take place between both—Kadambini wanted to prove that love was stronger from her side and Jogamaya wanted to prove that Kadambini did not reciprocate her love as she should. Either had no doubt that if they would ever meet by any chance none of them would be able to remain separated from each other for a single moment.

Kadambini told the gentleman, "I would like to go to Shripaticharan Babu's house in Nishindapur village."

---

* younger women are sometimes affectionely addressed as *Ma* or mother in Bengal by elders

The traveller was going to Calcutta, and though Nishindapur was not quite near, it fell on his way. He made the necessary arrangements himself and reached Kadambini to Shripaticharan's house.

The two friends met. They found it difficult to recognise each other for sometime but soon the resemblance to their childhood image of each other became clearer. Jogamaya said, "Oh My! What luck. I never thought I would ever get to meet you. But dear, how did you manage to come here? How come your in-laws allowed you to come?"

Kadambini stopped a while and then said, "Please dear, do not ask me about my in-laws. Do let me stay in one corner of your house, like a maid. I will work for you."

Jogamaya said, "Oh my! What are you saying, my dear? Why should you stay here like a maid? You are my dear friend.... my... ."

At this moment Shripati entered the room. Kadambini looked at his face for a moment and then slowly walked out of the room—she neither put on the veil covering her head nor did she exhibit any sign of shame or respect.

Jogamaya hurriedly began to explain the situation to Shripati in many ways lest he held any grudge against her friend. But she had to explain very little. Shripati agreed to her proposals so very easily that Jogamaya was not very pleased inwardly.

Kadambini did arrive at her friend's house, but somehow failed to associate freely with her—the valley of death seemed to come in between them. One cannot communicate with others when one loses faith in one's own self. Kadambini would look at Jogamaya's face and think so many things—think how her friend was living in a distant world apart, quite happy with her husband and her household. Jogamaya was associated with love, duties and affection—all the qualities of a worldly existence—whereas she herself was like a formless shadow. Jogamaya lived in the world of existence whereas she was existing as though eternity.

Jogamaya found this strange as well. She did not comprehend anything. A woman can never bear to live in mystery, for it was easy to poeticise uncertainty, glorify bravery, or add to one's store of knowledge, but to live with it in everyday homely existence was impossible. Thus a woman tends to erase the existence of that which she fails to understand and never keep any tie with it, or else create a new image of the same and try to make use of it; and if she failed to do both she would be quite annoyed with it.

The more complicated Kadambini turned out to be, Jogamaya grew more and more annoyed with her and grudge this new burden which had taken on her shoulders.

There was further trouble. Kadambini seemed to fear her own self. She was not able to flee from her own self. People who feared ghosts feared what was behind them all that which they could not see. But Kadambini was not afraid of what was outside for she feared the self within her the most.

Hence she would scream on lonely afternoons when she would be alone in her room—and her blood would curl when she would look at her own shadow created by the evening lamp.

Seeing Kadambini's strange fear, the rest of the household seemed to be seized by a kind of terror. The servants and maids, and even Jogamaya herself, began to see ghosts here and there every now and then.

Once it so happened that Kadambini ran crying out of her bedroom at midnight and knocked at Jogamaya's room door crying, "Didi, didi, I fall on your feet. Please do not leave me alone."

Jogamaya grew afraid and at the same time quite angry. She felt like driving out Kadambini that very instant, but the kind-hearted Shripati managed to calm her down and arranged shelter for Kadambini in the neighbouring room.

The next day Shripati was beckoned indoors at a very odd hour. Jogamaya chided him suddenly saying, "My dear, what kind of a man are you? A woman has left her in-laws' place and settled down in your house—it is almost a month now and she shows no signs of leaving—and still you do not utter a word of disapproval. Do explain what's in your mind? You men are all of one kind."

In fact, men do have an unjustified partiality towards the female species and are accused, primarily by women, for this. That Shripati's sympathy for this shelterless and beautiful Kadambini was a little more than the limits prescribed by society was quite evident in his behaviour, though he spoke to Jogamaya denying this vehemently.

He would think, "Perhaps this widow had been tortured unjustly by her in-laws and she could not bear it any longer and has ran away and taken shelter here. She has no parents, nor any one to call her own—how can I under such circumstances tell her to leave?" Hence he stayed away from finding out more information about her and neither had he any intention of hurting Kadambini by asking her about this unpleasant topic.

Thereafter, his wife began to harp upon his inert sense of duty in many ways. He understood very well that at least now he would have to inform Kadambini's in-laws in order to keep his own home peace intact. Ultimately he decided that writing a letter to them all of a sudden might bring undesirable results, hence he would go himself to Ranihaat to find out and then come to a serious conclusion.

When Shripati left Jogamaya came and told Kadambini, "Dear, your staying here is not very respectable. What will people say?"

Kadambini looked deeply at Jogamaya's face and said, "What relationship do I have with those people?"

Jogamaya was amazed, surprised. Angry, she asked, "You might not have, but we do. How can we keep a lady from another family forcibly?"

Kadambini said, "Where is my family?"

Jogamaya thought, "O Lord, what does this crazy woman say?"

Kadambini began to say softly, "Am I one of you? Or one of this world? You are laughing, crying, caring for each other, living with yourselves. I am only looking at you from a distance. You are human beings, I am only a shadow. I do not know why God has implanted me within your household. You fear that I would bring ill luck amidst your happiness, and I too do not fathom out what relationship I have with all of you. But as God has not constructed any other place for us and though the ties have broken we still move round you."

She spoke looking at her in such a way that Jogamaya felt she understood her more or less but she failed to comprehend the crux of the meaning and hence could not reply. She could not even ask a second time. So she went away in a deeply troubled state of mind.

IV

It was almost ten p.m. at night when Shripati returned from Ranihaat. The world was being washed by heavy rains. The continuous pitter-patter of the rains seemed to remind that this rain would never end, nor would this long night.

Jogamaya questioned, "What happened?" Shripati said, "There's lots to tell. I'll tell you later." Saying this he changed clothes, had his dinner, smoked tobacco and then went to bed. He looked worried.

Jogamaya had controlled her curiosity for long. She asked him as soon as she climbed the bed, "Now tell me what you've heard".

Shripati said, "You surely must have made a mistake."

Jogamaya was quite angry at this. Women could never make mistakes, and even if they did no wise man should ever mention it. They would do best to take it on their own shoulders. Jogamaya spoke in an annoyed voice, "How come?"

Shripati said, "The woman you have given shelter to cannot be your friend Kadambini."

It would anger anyone to hear of such a thing, and that too from one's husband. Jogamaya said, "That's really something. I do not know my childhood friend—you have to identify her to me. What are you hinting at?"

Shripati explained that now there could be no debate on what he was saying and that it was time to look at factual proof. There was no doubt that Jogamaya's friend Kadambini had died.

Jogamaya said, "Now just listen to that. You must have created severe confusion. God knows where you went and whom you have consulted? Who told you to go yourself, writing a letter would have cleared all the confusion."

Disappointed at his wife's scepticism regarding his efficiency, Shripati tried to point out logical details, but to no avail. Their arguments went on till midnight.

Though both agreed that Kadambini should be turned out of this house at that very instant since Shripati believed that his guest had cheated his wife by assuming a false identity, and Jogamaya believed that she had eloped from her home—none of them wanted to admit defeat.

Their voices soared higher, forgetting that Kadambini was lying in the next room.

One said, "What should I do now. I've heard it all myself," while another said in a firm voice, "How can I accept what you say, I've seen it all with my own eyes."

At last Jogamaya said, "Okay, then tell me when Kadambini had died." She thought she would pick out the date from one of Kadambini's old letters and point out the discrepancy in Shripati's news.

When both of them calculated the date it coincided with the date preceding the evening when Kadambini had come to their house. As soon as she heard this, Jogamaya's heart skipped a beat and Shripati too felt a similar sensation.

Just then the door opened and a fierce monsoon breeze extinguished the only lamp in the room. Darkness from without engulfed the room in a moment. Kadambini entered into the room and stood still. It was almost two and a half hours past midnight and raining incessantly outside.

Kadambini cried out, "My dear, I am the same Kadambini you knew, but now I am no longer alive. I am dead." Jogamaya shrieked out in fear, Shripati was dumbfounded.

"But what harm have I done besides being dead? I have nowhere to go in this living world nor in the world of the dead. Oh tell me where do I go?" With a sharp scream she seemed to wake up the sleeping gods in this deep rain-soaked night and ask, "Oh, Where do I go then?"

Exclaiming this she left the unconscious couple inside the dark room and went to find out her own shelter in the greater world outside.

V

It is difficult to say how Kadambini went back to Ranihaat. She never revealed herself in public. At first she stayed in the ruins of an old temple fasting the whole day.

When the untimely dark evening of a rainy day seemed to deepen and the villagers hurried to take shelter in their own homes fearing the approaching rough weather, Kadambini took to the streets. When she reached the main door of her in-laws' house her heart trembled, but as she drew the veil in full over her head and entered, the guards did not stop her mistaking her to be a maidservant. Around this time the rainfall worsened and the breeze blew speedily across.

At that hour the mistress of the house, Sharadashankar's wife, was playing cards with her widowed sister-in-law. The maid was busy in the kitchen and her child Khoka, who was sick, was sleeping in the bedroom. Kadambini escaped all eyes and entered that room. She did not know nor do I know why she had thought of visiting her in-laws' house. She only knew that she had to see Khoka once with her own eyes. Thereafter where she would go, what would happen—these questions had not come to her even once.

In the faint light of the lamp she saw the sickly, emaciated boy sleeping with his palms tightened. Seeing this her agitated heart grew anxious for affection—she fiercely desired to hold the boy with all his afflictions close to her heart and comfort him. And, then she remembered that as she was no longer there, who was to look after him? His mother loved his company chatting with him, playing with him but she had not taken any pains to bring up the child as she had been happy giving me that responsibility. But now who would look after him with the same care?

At that moment Khoka turned aside and spoke out in a semi-conscious state, "*Kakima*, give me water." "Oh my! So you have not forgotten your *Kakima**! My darling!" Kadambini hurriedly poured water from the clay pot, picked up Khoka on her chest and fed him water.

As long as he was in his sleep, Khoka did not think it strange to drink water from his *Kakima* as it had been his habit all along. But when *Kakima* kissed him fulfilling her long-cherished desire and put him to sleep once more, Khoka was wide awake. He hugged his dear aunt and asked, "*Kakima*, were you dead?"

Kakima answered, "Yes, Khoka."

"So you have come back to Khoka once again. Will you die again?"

Before she could reply there was a sudden commotion—the maid had entered with a bowl of

---

* wife of father's brother, an aunt

cereal, seeing her she let go of the bowl and fainted on the floor crying out "Oh My!"

The mistress of the house left her card game hearing the loud cry and came running. As soon as she entered the room she was dumbstruck and remained rooted to the spot, unable to utter a word.

Seeing all this, Khoka grew scared as well. He began to cry and said, "*Kakima* you go."

Kadambini had begun to feel that she was alive after a pretty long time. That old household and all its paraphernalia, that same Khoka, that affection she felt for him was all alive for her in the usual way—there had been no break of linkage between them nor had any kind of distance cropped up between them. She had felt that the childhood mate she had known had changed when she was staying with her friend; but when she entered Khoka's room she realised that Khoka's *Kakima* had not died a bit—she was still the same.

She anxiously cried out, "Didi, why are you fearing me? Look at me, I am still the very same woman you knew."

The mistress could not bear any longer and fell unconscious. Hearing of this story from his younger sister, Sharadashankar arrived at the interiors of the house himself. He pleaded Kadambini with folded hands, "*Chotobouma**, is this fair on your part? Satish is the only heir of our family, why are you casting an evil eye on him? Are we strangers to you? After you died, he has been growing thinner day by day and does not seem to recover from illness. He cries out '*Kakima, Kakima*' all the time. When you have left this world why

---

* the youngest daughter-in-law of a family addressed as such

don't you free yourself of all worldly ties? We will perform all the necessary rituals."

Kadambini could not bear his words any longer. She cried out intensely, "Please listen to me—I have not died. I have not died. How will I explain, I have not died. Look at this—I am still alive."

She picked up the brass bowl lying on the floor and hit her forehead violently—her forehead began to bleed profusely.

She said once more, "See, I am still alive."

Sharadashankar stood transfixed—Khoka began to call out to his father in fear and the two unconscious women lay on the floor.

Then, Kadambini, screaming "Please listen to me, I have not died, have not died, really I have not died", ran out of the room, descended the steps outside and plunged into the huge pool in the interiors of the house with a thud. Sharadashankar heard a loud splash from the room upstairs.

It rained the entire night, continued raining the next morning and even in the afternoon. There was no respite.

By dying, Kadambini had proved that she had not died.

✰✰✰✰✰

About the Book

'Mystic Moods' is a myriad collection of short stories evolving out of the mystique pen of Rabindranath Tagore. Through a very mystifying yet magnificient analysis of situations and characters Tagore has created universal narratives which remain forever alive. The sublimity with which he depicts futile human emotions, the desire to know the unknown and the fierce spirit of independence which breaks open all kinds of fetters, both social and psychological, perhaps remains unparalleled in literature. A certain distinctive mood personifies each of these ten short stories giving them a quaint flavour. This is what makes me call this collection 'Mystic Moods'.

About the Translator

Born in Calcutta in 1956 in an illustrious family of Shantiniketan, West Bengal, Sinjita Gupta did her post-graduation in English literature. She has been an English lecturer in several schools and colleges in Vizag, Mumbai and Delhi. Sinjita is the daughter of Late Prof. J M Sengupta, founder statistician of Indian Statistical Institute and niece of Late Shri Satyen Sen, freedom fighter, writer and winner of Sahitya Academy Award of Bangladesh. Her grandfather, Pandit Kshitimohan Sen, was the Vice-Chancellor of Viswabharati University and a close consort of Gurudev Rabindranath Tagore. Her family background and a childhood closely associated with Tagore's 'Shantiniketan' has contributed considerably to her present enterprise. As she says, this translation is like a 'dream come true' and a 'rediscovery of the great master's limitless greatness'.

Sinjita has to her credit several articles and short stories in *The Free Press Journal, Asian Age, Indian Express,* Mumbai, and *The New Nation Magazine,* Dacca, Bangladesh, besides several film reviews and critical essays. For two years she was the editor and coordinator of the Navy Wives Welfare Association's newsmagazine *Varuni*. She has organised, and performed in, social and cultural programmes, and taken part in debates, discussions and talks in The All India Radio. She has also appeared in interviews and women's programmes.

Her first book, *The Bauls of Bengal,* was published by Writers' Workshop, Kolkata. She is married to a senior naval officer and is currently residing in New Delhi.